IF WE DARE

Swoon Series

J.H. CROIX

IF WE DARE

Have you ever gone on a fake date? With your brother's best friend?

It all started when he rescued me from a dumpster. Not my best moment.

Grumpy, broody, too hot to handle Walker needs a date for a wedding. Let the complications begin.

———

It's not even a real date. I'm not even supposed to notice smokin' hot Jade. I don't believe in love, and weddings give me hives. Jade is smart and feisty, and she claims she's man-proof. She's perfect.

Perfect until we're stuck together for the weekend, and I can hardly keep my eyes, or my hands, off her. Perfect until I kiss her, and one kiss turns into so many more. And ***more***.

She stole the covers, and then she stole my heart.

One wedding. One weekend. Two hearts. It's all for show, right?

"A single act of kindness throws out roots in all directions, and the roots spring up and make new trees." -Amelia Earhart

Sign up for my newsletter for information on new releases & get a FREE copy of one of my books!

http://jhcroixauthor.com/subscribe/

Follow me!
jhcroix@jhcroix.com
https://www.bookbub.com/authors/j-h-croix
https://www.facebook.com/jhcroix
https://www.instagram.com/jhcroix/

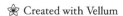 Created with Vellum

Chapter One

JADE

"Hey!" I called, my eyes trained on the jerk who was getting a little too handsy with a woman at the bar. I'd served her and her friends a few minutes ago, and tonight was her twenty-first birthday.

The woman in question, Megan something or other, tried to laugh it off, politely taking a few steps away. It was crowded in the bar tonight, though, so there wasn't far for her to go. The man immediately closed the space between them.

"Hey!" I called, quickly lifting a section of the counter at the back of the bar, slipping out, and aiming right for the group where they were standing.

Megan wasn't alone, but her friends were tied up flirting. Striding up to the man, I tapped him on the shoulder. He turned back, a leer affixed to his face. "Oh, hey, hot bartender, what can I do for you?" he slurred.

I silently cursed the other bartender on duty tonight, Joe, who tended not to pay too much attention to just how drunk people were getting and continued to serve them anyway. That was a problem for another evening, though.

Narrowing my eyes as I looked up at the lumbering jerk standing before me, I rested a hand on my hip. "Back the fuck off. It doesn't look like she appreciates your attention."

Megan's eyes met mine—I only knew her name because I'd carded her—relief passing across her face. "Thank you," she mouthed.

"Since when do you speak for all women?" The man punctuated this sentence with a long burp, which got a few guffaws from his friends surrounding him.

I cast a sharp gaze amongst the group. I had no problem throwing every single one of these guys out. "Like I said, back off. Consider this my last warning."

The asshole *still* didn't get it. He leaned down, getting a little too close to my face, and slurred. "Fuck off. Get back behind the bar and serve my friends some drinks."

Perhaps I should've been afraid, but I wasn't. For starters, the bar-back and Joe were around and nearby. I also had friends here tonight, even if they didn't happen to be in this precise corner of the sprawling Lost Deer Bar where I was only covering a shift as a favor tonight.

"That does it. You're out of here," I said, gesturing over my shoulder toward the door as I reached for the guy's arm.

"Hell no! I'm not fucking leaving," he grumbled, reaching for poor Megan, who was pinned against the wall at this point, doing her best to look invisible. He snatched her hand. Well, fuck it.

Ignoring the rumble of voices around me, I lifted my boot and kicked him right in the knee. I decided to go for that instead of his balls as a starting point. In the back of my mind, I was legitimately wondering where the hell my help was.

The guy cried out in pain. His broad face turned a mottled red as he dropped Megan's hand—that was my goal, so I took that as a win—and stepped toward me. Next thing I knew, he'd grabbed me by the waist with both hands and heaved me in the air.

I didn't scare easy, but now a little bit of fear bolted through me. I was known for getting myself in a pickle here and there, and I just might've gone and done that now.

Before I could make a peep, a voice came over my shoulder. "Put her down. Now."

Whoever spoke wasn't waiting. Next thing I knew, a hand shot out, slamming into the guy's elbow. Something happened to the guy's knees too. He stumbled and cried out sharply. Just as I began to tumble loose from his hold, my savior caught me with one arm and pulled me against his side.

I glanced up into the face of Walker Hudson. My body felt as if a live wire had grazed me and left me humming with electricity. With Walker holding me fast to his side with one arm, I wasn't going anywhere. I might not've liked it in my mind, but my body thought it was freaking awesome. Walker was nothing but pure muscle and lean power as he held me close.

The jerk who'd grabbed me was still groaning about his knee, but gathered himself together enough to glare at Walker. "You fucking dick."

He made a move toward Walker, who simply lifted one arm and grabbed him by the wrist. Whatever he did brought the man to his knees with a yelp.

"Now, you're gonna fucking leave before I kick your ass," Walker said.

His low, fierce words sent a sizzling thrill through me. I was *not* the kind of girl who got all hot and bothered over men being tough. And yet, here I was, my body nearly vibrating at the force of Walker's presence and my panties getting wet from the sound of his voice.

I stole another glance at him. I knew him because he worked with my older brother, and they were friends. To put it plainly, Walker was hot. His face looked as if it had been carved from marble. He had strong cheekbones and a straight nose paired with a square jaw. He even had a dimple in his chin. To make matters worse, his lips were bold and sensual.

I didn't think I'd ever seen the guy crack a smile. His eyes were an icy silver. Ever since the first time I'd met Walker, we'd rubbed each other the wrong way. For God's sake, the man was all about being tall, dark, and mysterious. It grated on me, and I didn't know why.

Not that I minded that issue just about now. He leveled his cool gaze at the guy's friends, adding, "Why don't y'all get the hell out of here? Sound like a plan?"

Whether it was the tone of his voice, or the look in his eyes, or the fact that whatever he'd done to the guy with a flick of his wrist had brought the guy to his knees, they took notice. After a loaded moment, the man's friends appeared to think Walker's suggestion was a good plan and started to shuffle out.

"Are we clear?" Walker asked, staring down at my drunken assailant on his knees.

"If you'll fucking let me go, I'll get the hell out of here."

Walker released the guy's wrist. "Fair enough. If I ever see you getting pushy with any woman who doesn't want it, I might not be so nice next time."

At that, the man stood, stumbling on his way toward the door, which was blessedly close. Only then did Walker glance down at me. He eased his hold on me, releasing me from that convenient little spot tucked up against his hard body.

I jumped back and eyed him carefully. I wanted to tell him I didn't need his help, but I wasn't stupid. I knew the second I was lifted off the floor, I had no chance against the drunk man. I took a breath, willing my pulse to slow the hell down and every cell in my body to stop it with the happy dance.

"Thank you. I should've kicked him in the balls first," I finally said.

Walker's lips quirked in a smile, immediately sending my belly into a series of flips. "That might've done the trick."

Megan jumped in. "Thank you so much. He was so drunk, and he just wouldn't leave me alone."

"I don't know if you should be thanking me," I said wryly.

"Well, thank you both. I'm going to take that as my cue to call it a night." At that, she waved at us both and hurried through the crowd to sidle up to one of her friends.

That left me alone with Walker. I was acutely aware of my pulse, its thrumming beat careening through my body at a breakneck pace. "What did you do to his wrist?" I couldn't help my curiosity.

He shrugged. "Just applied some well-placed pressure to a pressure point."

"Well, um, thanks again. I'm not sure where Joe went—"

Walker chuckled at that. "Oh, he's making out with some girl in the back."

"What? You have got to be fucking kidding me," I muttered.

"I'm definitely not kidding. You can see him," he said, nudging his chin toward the swinging half door that led behind the bar to the kitchen and storage.

Glancing over my shoulder, I saw Walker was quite right. Joe was deep into making out with a woman against the wall in the hallway. I was actually relieved to have something else to be annoyed about. I didn't know what to think about my body's haywire reaction to getting up close and personal with Walker, so any distraction was welcome.

"I have to get back to work, so thanks again," I said, giving him a nod. As if to remind me that while I might be trying to ignore it, my body knew what it wanted. My belly shimmied as I strode quickly past him and stepped behind the bar again.

Chapter Two

WALKER

Jade Cole practically ran past me, and my eyes were like a magnet on her, tracking every step. Her glossy dark hair fell like a river down her back, the long tresses catching the light and swinging as she moved. I couldn't help but think how it would feel to spin that glorious hair around my fist.

Only Jade—barely up to my chin and maybe a third of the size of the drunk guy she'd taken on—would think it made sense to try to kick him out like that on her own. But then, Jade didn't strike me as the kind of girl to ever back down.

As I turned to walk away, it didn't slip my notice that the side of my body where I'd pulled her close felt like it was on fire. Jade was a petite bundle of curves with enough sass and spirit to tempt me beyond all reason.

With a mental shake, I walked away, telling myself to remember all the reasons why I'd avoided spending much time alone with Jade. I had once spent roughly fifteen minutes in the car alone with her when I gave her a ride home. That short span of time had made me question whether I'd previously understood what the concept of chemistry meant. Chemistry between two people, that is. I didn't quite know how it was possible, but the space in my car during that time felt as if lightning had struck, every particle in the air vibrating from its lingering power.

Riiiiight. I didn't need to wonder what Jade might be doing tonight after the bar closed, most definitely not.

I returned to the booth where I'd stopped to catch a few drinks with the guys on my first responder crew. Dawson, as usual, was cracking jokes. Jade's brother Lucas was nowhere to be found. Most likely because that man was about as head over heels in love as a man could be with his girlfriend, Valentina.

Slipping into the booth, I took a long drag on my beer, glancing over when I heard my name. "What?"

"Well, look at that. He speaks," Dawson teased.

I rolled my eyes. "Of course. You've heard me speak plenty of times."

"Well, you were Jade's savior there. I was commenting that will further the legend," he said.

"Huh? What legend?" I asked cautiously as I glanced around the table.

Wade waggled his eyebrows. "Ever since you rescued that girl from the climbing accident a few weeks back, she's been spreading rumors about how hot you are and how you're the best rescuer." He added air quotes around the word best.

"What? I was just doing my job. All of y'all have rescued people. This is not just a me thing."

Jackson winked and shrugged. "She's got the hots for you. It'll blow over. Plus, you're still considered new around here, so you're more exciting than the rest of us."

"What the hell? I've lived here for six months," I muttered.

Dawson chuckled. "Six months is nothing. People are nosy. Plus, you're single."

"That's how I like it. I plan to keep it that way," I replied.

"That's only going to make you enigmatic," Wade offered.

"A-plus for vocabulary," Dawson chimed in with a wink.

"Fuck enigmatic. There's no mystery about me. I mind my own business," I countered.

I did, in fact, mind my own business. I also had zero interest in romance. I'd been there, done that, and found it a waste of time. I was all fucking set with romance.

The night meandered along. I decided to cut out early, if only because I was legitimately tired. Between some training that morning on a climbing wall and a hiking rescue that afternoon, I was ready to try to catch some shut-eye.

Stepping out into the cool spring darkness, I paused to stare at the sky for a few beats. Clouds drifted in front of the half moon, stars glittering in between them. The mountain ridge ahead was silhouetted in the darkness with a silver shaft of moonlight angling across part of it.

Lowering my gaze, I began walking toward my truck. A scuffing sound drew my attention. I didn't see anyone in the parking lot until my eyes landed on the dumpster in the far corner.

The moment I noticed the silhouette of the bottom perched at the top of the dumpster, I knew I was staring at Jade Cole's luscious ass.

She was kicking her legs. I didn't know how, but she seemed stuck. My boots moved toward her. My greedy eyes took the moment to absorb the sight of her. *Cut the shit*, my good angel said. *She's not on display personally for you.*

"Jade?" I stopped beside the dumpster, puzzling about how she got herself half stuck in the dumpster.

"Walker?" she returned, her tone slightly surprised.

"Yep, that would be me. Need some help?"

"Does it look like I need help?" she countered swiftly, her annoyance clear.

I bit back a laugh. "I'm not quite sure because I'm

guessing you would jump down. But you're not trying, so something's up."

Stepping closer, I peered over the edge of the dumpster to investigate. Nothing was immediately evident. "Uh, I'm not sure how I can help."

"I got caught," she muttered, reaching her hand toward her waist.

Tracking her motion, I noticed her belt loop had snagged on a hook sticking out inside the edge of the dumpster.

"Damn. Stop wiggling, Jade. That nail's rusty and you're gonna scratch yourself if you're not careful."

"Tell me something I don't know, genius," she retorted.

"How attached are you to that belt loop?" I asked as I leaned over to peer closer.

Jade turned her head to the side, somehow managing to be sexy as hell even though she was in a decidedly awkward position.

"Not at all. I already tried to tear it, but no luck."

Sliding my hand in my pocket, I pulled out the small pocket knife I kept on me at all times for no particular reason, except for the fact that it came in handy time and again. Flipping it open, I stepped closer to her hips. "I'm gonna cut it, okay?"

"Of course, cut away. And, of course you have a pocket knife. You're *that* kind of guy."

I chuckled as I pressed my hand against her hip, just enough to lift it slightly so I could get a better view of where her belt loop was hitched on the hook. In another second, I sliced clean through it. She started to wiggle down, beginning to come down sideways.

Dropping the knife, I caught her in the nick of time as she stumbled to the ground when one of her cowboy boots struck the pavement. "Easy," I murmured as I steadied her.

Jade straightened, lifting a hand and brushing a few locks of hair out of her eyes. She blew a puff of air to send the last errant lock off her forehead. Stepping back, she sighed. "Thank you. I guess I owe you twice now."

"You don't owe me. I did what anyone would do."

Jade's gaze was considering as she stared at me in the parking lot with moonlight gilding her hair in silver. "Actually, that's not true. That asshole got going in the bar and you were the only person who even noticed. Plus, not everyone carries a pocket knife everywhere," she said, her tone dry.

I felt my lips kick up on one side. "I suppose not. Maybe it's none of my business, but what the hell were you doing climbing into the dumpster anyway?"

"When I threw the trash bag in, one of my bracelets flew off my wrist," she explained, gesturing to her now bare wrist.

I couldn't say I'd considered it much, but I was aware she usually wore a wide silver bracelet on her wrist. I shouldn't have known that detail, but then every detail about Jade appeared to be burned into my brain without any effort on my part.

"Well, then we should find it. Tell me what it looks like." Without thinking further, I curled a hand on the side of the dumpster and jumped in.

Jade's usual guarded expression, for once, subsided. Her eyes went wide and her mouth fell open. "Tell me what it looks like," I repeated.

She snapped her mouth shut, a wondering laugh escaping. There I stood, in the fucking dumpster, mind you, and the sound of her throaty laugh elicited a low pull in my gut. Much as I preferred not to want Jade, I did. As much as I needed air to breathe, my body wanted Jade. Which was why I generally avoided her.

"It's silver," she finally said. "About this wide." She held up two fingers to demonstrate.

Glancing down to where my boots were planted amongst garbage bags, I scanned for a glimpse of silver. When the moon and the dim light in the far corner of the parking lot didn't do me any favors, I slipped my phone out of my pocket and tapped the flashlight button. Once the bright light came on, I moved it in a pattern over the trash bags, my eyes stopping when the light reflected off something.

I walked a few steps over and reached down into the not-so-pleasant smelling trash. "Got it," I called, holding the bracelet aloft.

When I straightened, Jade, who didn't smile very often, graced me with a beauty. Her lips curled at the corners as her smile unfurled and her eyes tilted. "Wow! You found it."

Stepping back to the edge of the dumpster, I handed it to her before resting one hand on the edge and hopping over to land on the pavement beside her. Jade spun the bracelet in a circle in her hands, still smiling. This time when her gaze met mine, it was almost shy. "That was really sweet, Walker."

Oh hell. "Sweet" was not an adjective I was usually labeled with. I felt an unbidden smile tugging up the corners of my mouth.

"Well, now I owe you three times. Don't argue the point," she said quickly when I opened my mouth to do exactly that.

I did the craziest thing next. "Actually, if you insist, I do have a favor I could use some help with."

"Anything."

"I have to go to a wedding, and I could use a date." I couldn't believe I actually said that, but the words were out, so there was no going back.

For the second time in my experience, Jade's mouth fell open. After an electrifying moment of silence, she asked, "A date?"

Maybe I hadn't thought too much about this, or not at all, but I wasn't one to back down. "Yep. A date."

She rested a hand on her hip. "Is this a joke?"

I shook my head slowly, a plan materializing in my brain. "Definitely not. Next weekend. A good friend of mine is getting married, and I'd rather not go solo." Just as I began to think that I didn't want to have to explain why to Jade, her question sliced through the pause.

"And why not? You're not exactly the kind of man who can't handle a wedding on his own."

I decided right then and there that I was going to dive into this insanity. I had an itch to scratch, a quite specific itch. She could be my date for the weekend, and we could burn this fire between us to ashes.

If I had to explain why, then so be it. "Look, it's one of my best buds. I was going to go without a date and say fuck it all, but my ex is going to be there."

"You have an ex?" Jade interjected, arching a brow so high, I was surprised it didn't fly off her forehead.

"Yes. I have an ex. We broke up because she screwed around on me with my best friend's brother. I'm not sure what's up, but she's been texting and calling lately. I get the idea she wants another chance. I'd rather her not get *any* ideas," I said flatly. I didn't feel much of anything about it and was more than glad to close the door on that whole mess. It was just I preferred not to have any pitying gazes cast my way during the wedding, and I definitely preferred my ex to consider me off-limits. It would be easier to convey that message if she thought I was dating someone.

Several things flashed through Jade's eyes, ending with them narrowing in anger. "Oh, that's *not* cool. I'm guessing the brother will be at the wedding."

I nodded. "Yeah. It's his family. I'm well over my ex, before you worry that's what this is about. But, I'd prefer for her to leave me alone."

"I'm your girl," Jade said, nodding vigorously.

"Okay then. Sounds like we have a plan. Can you handle a long weekend out of town—three days?"

"I'll make sure I can. I'll be the best date you ever had, and I'll make her feel like the cheating bitch she is."

I couldn't help but laugh. "Tell me where to pick you up. It's next weekend."

"Here, let me give you my number. Just text me the details. I'll rearrange my schedule and you'll have me." When she said it *that* way, every cell in my body thought *having* her would be perfect. "By the way," Jade continued, her voice cutting through my train of thought. "I would've done this even if you hadn't saved my ass from that fool and then gotten me out of the dumpster and found my bracelet. It's just the principle, you know?"

"Oh, I do."

After I entered Jade's number in my phone, I watched as she strolled back into the bar. Her cowboy boots struck on the gravel with each step and her hair swung at her waist. Electricity sizzled up my spine. Three days with Jade was going to be interesting.

Chapter Three

JADE

"You're what?" Valentina asked from where she sat at the kitchen table in the house she shared with my older brother.

"I'm going to be Walker's date for the wedding. His ex screwed around on him with his best friend's brother. That is *so* not cool."

Reflexively, I glanced over my shoulder to see if Lucas happened to be approaching. Lucas was long over what happened with his late wife. Hell, he hadn't even found out until after she died, which in a way made it all worse. He was stumbling through grief over her death and found out she'd been screwing around.

Valentina—the love of his life and as far I was concerned the best woman *ever* for him—gave me a wide-eyed look. "I can't imagine pulling that off."

"Don't worry. I took drama in high school, and I am committed to this. It's personal."

"What, did someone screw around on you?" Valentina asked as she leaned forward to snag her cup of coffee.

"No, but after what Lucas went through, it's a sore point for me."

"Oh gosh, Lucas is doing fine," Valentina replied, brushing her curly hair off her shoulders.

Valentina was almost too beautiful. She had dark red hair that fell in curls around her shoulders and wide blue eyes. She had this ridiculously beautiful skin with freckles scattered like gold glitter on her cheeks. Lucas had fallen for her so hard it was ridiculous. Despite her beauty, that wasn't what I cared about. Valentina adored Lucas and was loyal to the bone.

"Of course he's doing fine. He's got you," I said. "He's no longer in the running to win a gold medal for being a broody asshole. For that, I will forever be grateful. You're the sunshine in his life, and I'm not even kidding when I say that."

Valentina flashed a shy grin. "All right then. I'm just trying to picture anyone spending the weekend with Walker. Walker's kinda, I don't know, quiet."

"Yeah, he's kinda like Lucas used to be after he got screwed over."

Chapter Four

WALKER

"Who did you say you're bringing with you to that wedding?" Jackson asked, the skepticism evident in his tone.

"Jade," I replied before adjusting the air gun I held in my hand and giving the nail a final tap.

We were in the middle of installing wide plank hardwood flooring in a new guest cabin on the grounds where I worked at Stolen Hearts Lodge. I held my hand out, expecting to feel another piece of wood laid in my palm. When I didn't, I glanced up to find Jackson staring at me, his mouth slightly open and one hand on his hip.

I wiggled my fingers. He let out a rough laugh before leaning over and handing me another piece of flooring. I fit the piece of wood into the grooves of the last row before reaching for the air gun and quickly nailing the board into place.

"Have you lost your damn mind?" Jackson asked.

"Not that I'm aware of," I replied as I straightened. "Why do you ask?"

"You know Jade is Lucas's sister, right?" Jackson paused

to snag a water bottle sitting on the edge of the miter saw stand nearby.

I took my leather work gloves off and reached for a water bottle on the unfinished windowsill by my elbow. Turning, I leaned my hips against it as I drained the half empty bottle. "Yeah, I know she's Lucas's sister," I replied as I spun the now empty bottle in my palm. "It's not a real date. It's a fake date."

Jackson lowered his water slowly, running a hand through his shaggy brown curls as he eyed me dubiously. "A fake date? Is that a real thing?"

"You're asking me if a fake date is real?" At Jackson's nod, I couldn't help but laugh. "In this case, yes, it is."

Jackson shook his head slowly. "Dude, that's fucked up. I have so many questions. For starters, why do you have a fake date? Then, how did this conversation even come about? Does Lucas know?"

A voice carried from the open doorway. "And how the hell did you get Jade Cole to agree to that date?" Dawson asked as he stepped into the semi-finished cabin.

Jackson threw his head back with a laugh. "I was about to get to that question."

Jackson Stone was my boss at Stolen Hearts Lodge and owned the outdoor adventure lodge. He also happened to be a veterinarian and had a clinic on site, which was handy since there was also a rescue program for animals here. Dawson also worked here and was on the Stolen Hearts Valley Emergency Response crew with both Jackson and me. I'd snapped up this job when I saw it about six months ago.

For the most part, I liked my job. The lodge was one of those places where everyone was friends with everyone. I didn't mind that so much. But most everyone here was nosy. Even the guys.

I looked between Jackson and Dawson and asked, "Where should I start?"

Dawson's face broke into a wide smile. He shrugged easily, his eyes glinting with mirth. "Take your pick, man."

Jackson chuckled and drained his water before leveling me with his gaze. "What the fuck, dude?"

"I'll keep it brief. I needed a favor. Jade offered. Y'all saw when I stepped in the middle of that scene at Lost Deer Bar the other night and got that asshole who'd picked her up off the floor away from her. When Jade said she owed me one, I decided to take her up on it. So yeah, it's a real fake date. She's just doing me a favor."

"But why the hell do you need a fake date to your friend's wedding?" Jackson asked.

Dawson crossed his arms in front of his chest, his lips kicking up in a slight grin. With my friends eyeing me curiously, I shifted my shoulders. "Look, I guess it is a little strange. See, my ex is going to be at the wedding. It's not that I can't deal with her. Before you go thinking otherwise, I'm over her. Out of nowhere the last month or so, she started texting and calling me again. She's dating my friend's brother, and I'm getting the vibe she's looking for a way out. I do *not* want to deal with her bullshit, so it'll be easier if I have a date."

Dawson nodded slowly, cocking his head to the side. "Why the hell is your ex going to be at your best friend's wedding? I mean, he's your best friend, right?"

Jesus. These guys and their fucking questions.

"Yeah," I replied with a sigh, pausing to toss my empty water bottle into the recycling bin we had in the corner. "She screwed around on me with his brother. His brother is a fucking dick. If Dave had his way, his brother wouldn't even be at his wedding, but you know how that shit goes with family."

"Oh, for fuck's sake," Jackson muttered. "Now that's a bunch of bullshit. Under those circumstances, I get finding yourself a fake date."

"But how the hell did you get Jade to say yes?" Dawson

interjected, looping back to his original question when he entered the room.

I shrugged. "I asked her. She said yes, probably because I helped her out the other night. Is that so surprising?"

Dawson arched a brow, nodding slowly. Jackson nodded right along with him, prompting me to ask, "What's the big deal?"

"Jade doesn't date." Jackson made that comment firmly.

"Maybe she said yes because it's not a real date," I offered, wanting to ask more about exactly why Jade didn't date. I kept my mouth shut with those questions because I didn't want to drag them further into my business than they already were.

"I guess so," Dawson said with a light shrug. "But you never did tell us, does Lucas know?"

"I don't know. I suppose I should tell him." God help me. All of this was starting to seem complicated. I hated complications.

"Well, yeah, you gotta tell him," Jackson said, as if this was obvious.

"Jade *is* his little sister," Dawson added.

My impulsive invitation for Jade to join me at the wedding was snowballing with complications. "Fuck. Do I need to worry about Lucas getting pissed off? It's not a real date."

Jackson shrugged. "Don't think so. I would just let him know you have a fake date. Otherwise, maybe he'll think it's real," he said with a slow grin.

"Okay, fill me in on why the hell Jade doesn't date," I said, giving into some of my curiosity.

Jackson and Dawson shrugged in unison. "Hell if I know," Dawson offered. "All I know is one of the other bartenders tried to ask her out and she told him to fuck off, that she didn't date. She's kind of private."

"Like you," Jackson offered with a chuckle.

"For fuck's sake. I might have to cancel the fake date if I'm gonna have to deal with all this crap."

Dawson clapped me on the shoulder. "Too late. Plus, this is a good story. I can't wait to hear how the wedding goes."

"Fine, fine," I muttered as I turned and picked up my work gloves from where I'd set them on the windowsill. "What are you doing out here anyway? I didn't think you were working today."

"Oh right. Came out to check with you guys about the schedule for the crew. I need to go out of town in two weeks. Can one of you cover for me?"

"I got it," I replied quickly. "You can cover for me when I'm at the wedding."

"When's that?"

"Next weekend."

"You've got a deal, man," Dawson replied with a nod. "Just so you know, I'd cover for you anyway." He pushed away from the doorframe with another grin and a wink. "Catch y'all later." He stepped back through the open doorway with a wave.

Jackson and I got back to work, and I resisted the urge to ask any further questions about Jade. My curiosity about her was steadfast and rising. I made a mental note to check on the room situation at the hotel.

Chapter Five

JADE

"What?" Lucas asked. My older brother punctuated his question with a whip of his head in my direction and one of his dark brows slashing up.

Shocked was the only way to describe his one-word question. I picked up a slice of apple covered in peanut butter—my niece's afternoon snack—and popped it in my mouth as I nodded.

"You're going to a wedding with Walker?" Lucas asked slowly. He slid his hand over the counter, brushing away crumbs from the sandwiches he'd been assembling for Rylie, his daughter and my adorable niece. Turning, he dusted his hands over the trashcan and leaned his hips against the counter as he surveyed me.

"Yeah, that's what I said. Is that a problem? And why are you looking at me like that?"

Lucas cocked his head to the side, his green eyes, so similar to mine, narrowing. "Uh, maybe because I can't remember the last time you went on a date. Not to mention, a wedding seems kind of like a big event. I'm guessing you left out the fact that you and Walker have been dating for a

while. I'm so confused I'm not even sure if I should be
pissed off at him."

"Oh my God, Lucas. You're totally overreacting." I shook
my head slowly. "It's not a real date. It's a fake date. He
needs a favor, so I told him I'd help out."

Lucas gave his head a shake. "A fake date?"

"What's a fake date?" Rylie asked as she came bouncing
into the living room adjacent to the kitchen. She skipped her
way over to me before snatching up a slice of apple with
peanut butter and popping it in her mouth.

"That's a very good question," Lucas said.

I bit back a sigh. I suppose I should've explained better
and considered that my ever curious niece might appear with
nosy questions.

"Okay. It's a date, but we're not dating. Romantically
speaking," I explained.

Rylie finished chewing and leaned over to reach for the
napkins in the center of the table. I stretched my arm out,
nudging the stack in her direction. After wiping her mouth,
she angled her head to the side. Like Lucas and me, Rylie
had almost black hair and green eyes. Unlike me, her hair
had a bit of a curl to it like her father's.

Rylie narrowed her eyes and pursed her lips. "I don't
understand," she said, her solemn tone almost making me
laugh aloud.

"Walker's a friend," I said, looking between them. "He
did me a favor the other night and helped me out with a
situation at the bar. I told him I'd be happy to return the
favor. He needs a date to a wedding, so I'm going."

This was all starting to seem rather ridiculous. Plus, I
couldn't explain it completely in front of Rylie. What had
tipped my hand to agree was learning that Walker's ex had
screwed around on him and would be at the wedding. After
what Rylie's mother had done to Lucas, well, I had feelings
about that kind of thing. I couldn't exactly discuss that in
front of Rylie.

Rylie wrinkled her nose and grinned. "That's weird."

"Walker's a friend. Just like I would go somewhere with Valentina because she's my friend, I'll do the same for Walker," I explained.

That explanation finally seemed to satisfy Rylie. Her attention shifted to her father. "Can I go outside?"

Lucas nodded. "You know the rules."

With a squeal, Rylie dashed to the side of the kitchen. The screen door bounced behind her, and she skipped out into the yard, immediately heading over to the small tree house a few feet off the ground. Lucas had built that for her last month, and she loved it.

Lucas watched as she disappeared into the tiny space before his gaze slid back to me. "Okay, what's really going on? I couldn't believe it when Walker mentioned he was taking you to the wedding."

I threw my hands up. "*Nothing* is going on. Like nothing. You weren't there, but Walker stepped in and broke up a bit of a scuffle at the bar the other night. This asshole was getting out of hand with a girl there for her twenty-first birthday. You know me—"

I paused when Lucas muttered, "Oh, I know you."

"What do you mean?"

"Just that you never back down from a confrontation. Sometimes I worry about you because of that."

With a roll of my eyes, I continued, "Anyway, I tried to get him to back off and the guy was drunk enough that he grabbed me. Walker intervened and straightened things out. When he said he needed a date for the wedding, and I found out it was because his ex screwed around on him with his best friend's brother, well, I'm all on board." I left out the bit about Walker helping me out of the dumpster and finding my bracelet. Lucas didn't need to know every freaking detail.

Lucas chuckled softly. "And what exactly are you going to do?"

"Make her fucking regret it," I said flatly.

"No need to take what happened with Melissa personally, Jade." Lucas was referring to his late wife who died from an aneurysm. We found out after she died that she'd cheated on him with a friend for over a year. "In case you missed it, I've more than moved on. Valentina's the best thing that ever happened to me."

"I know you have," I said with a sigh. "Valentina is amazing and I adore her. But, I owe Walker a favor. If he needs a date to that wedding, I'll do it. It's totally platonic, so don't read anything into it."

Lucas studied me, his gaze speculative. I crossed my legs, my thumb reflexively reaching to my opposite wrist to trace over the silver bracelet I wore there, the very bracelet Walker had rescued for me.

"I thought you didn't date," he said with a subtle lift of his chin and the hint of a dare in his tone.

I lifted my own chin in return, meeting his gaze head-on. "I don't. Like I told you, this isn't a real date. It's not like that."

He angled his head to the side, staying quiet just long enough that I shifted my shoulders and uncrossed my legs only to cross the other leg over the top again.

"You know, you had an opinion on my lack of a love life before I met Valentina," Lucas commented, his tone casual.

"So what if I did?" I managed in reply, clinging to the steely defiance that got me through most situations when I felt uncomfortable. Unfortunately for me, my brother wasn't intimidated and knew me better than just about anyone else.

"I'm just sayin'," he drawled, "you gave me a lecture on how I should give someone a chance. Think you said something about keeping my options open, or some other nonsense like that."

"And? Look where it got you. You found Valentina. She's amazing and we all adore her."

Lucas smiled slowly. "I did. And I just might be the luckiest man in the world. My love life isn't the topic of conversation right now. Yours is. Or lack thereof, I should say."

I took a breath, willing the churning in my gut to stop. "I'm perfectly fine without any love life. Society places expectations on women, and I'm happy without anyone. I don't need any pressure, much less from you," I snapped.

Lucas's gaze sobered quickly. "Hey, I didn't mean to hit a sore spot. You know I've got your back."

Few people knew much about one spectacularly shitty event in my life. Lucas was on the shortlist. He *did* have my back. I loved him all the more for it.

The silver bracelet on my wrist was warming up with my thumb sliding over it mindlessly. My foot bounced, discharging all that restless energy hanging around inside me.

"Walker is a good guy," Lucas said, out of nowhere as far as I was concerned.

"I know. He's been around town long enough. All of you in the crew sure like him, so I trust him. You don't need to go all big brother on me."

My brother's far too piercing green gaze held mine. "I'm not going big brother on you, whatever the fuck that means. I just didn't know what to think when Walker saw fit to tell me he was taking you away for a weekend. Case you were wondering, he explained it was a fake date. Or, as Jackson put it, a real fake date," Lucas said.

I didn't want to think about why Lucas made the point that Walker was a nice guy. Nor did I want to contemplate just how sexy Walker was. Which I did every single time he came to mind. He was all man wrapped up in a package of tall, dark, and broody.

If I had a type—which I totally didn't—it wasn't him. No matter what my body thought when he happened to be in proximity.

Chapter Six

WALKER

Jade lived right down the street from me. I knew this because I'd given her a ride home once last winter after she got a flat tire. I'd forgotten just how electric the small space in my truck felt for those roughly fifteen minutes from Stolen Hearts Lodge to her place.

I told myself that was probably a fluke, something to do with the weather and the fact I'd been in a melancholic space right before the holidays. Last winter had been my family's first holiday season without my father since he'd passed away. He went in the best way possible. According to the doctor he had a massive heart attack in his sleep. Mind you, I'm not saying heart attacks are a good thing. Just making the point that he lived a full life and if he was going to go, why not go like that? Quick and clean. No matter what, we all missed the hell out of him.

I forced my thoughts back to the present as I turned the steering wheel into Jade's driveway. She had a cute little house, practically out of a postcard. It was a small two-story house with gabled windows upstairs and a peaked roof with bright purple shutters. It was late spring with the flowers in full bloom in her yard. The scent of honeysuckle drifted around me as I walked past a cluster of it running along the side of her driveway.

Through text, we'd agreed I would pick her up this afternoon. The wedding was north of here at a winery and hotel in the mountains. We needed to arrive with enough time to prep for tonight's wedding rehearsal dinner. Jade had assured me she was more than ready to pull off an "epic" performance. That was her description, and I didn't even know what to think. Beyond the question about just what the hell we were doing, I'd begun to wonder if this was such a good idea.

Stepping onto the small porch, which had flower boxes on the railings, I knocked lightly on the purple door. I distantly heard Jade calling in return, "Be there in a sec!"

As I waited, I let my gaze scan the mountain range in the distance. We had roughly an hour and a half drive ahead of us into Virginia where the landscape would be similar. The Appalachian Mountains stretched all the way up the East Coast. For now, the legendary blue haze over the mountains was shot through by the late afternoon sunshine, giving it a silvery halo. Although I hadn't grown up specifically in Stolen Hearts Valley, I'd grown up a mere hour away in the Blue Ridge Mountains, and these views were home to me.

At the sound of the door opening behind me, I turned back. The moment my eyes landed on Jade, my body tightened. To my point of wondering if this was a good idea. I was seriously doubting the wisdom of spending a weekend with Jade.

Her midnight hair fell loose around her shoulders. Her rich green eyes met mine, a sly glint in them. "Are we ready?"

My confusion must've shown on my face because she clarified. "You know"—she circled her hand in the air—"to go to the wedding and make your ex look like the bitch she is."

Jade appeared a little too excited about this, but I

couldn't help but laugh. I shrugged. "You know, it doesn't have to be a big deal."

Jade rested a hand on her hip, tapping the toe of one of her cowboy boots on the hardwood floor in her entryway. "Oh, yes, it does. I get your point. You're over her, but there'd be more questions if you showed up alone while she's there with the groom's brother. I just prefer to make her regret it." This was punctuated with a hard roll of Jade's eyes.

I chuckled again. "Yes, I'm ready. Do you need me to carry anything?"

Jade shook her head, turning to fetch a bag to the side of the door. She stepped out, shooing my hand away when I reached for her bag. "I got it."

She walked at my side along the slate flagstones to where my truck was parked in the circular driveway. Her small hatchback was parked in front of the garage doors. She stopped in the gravel driveway. "Should I put my bag in the back?" She gestured toward the covered back of my truck.

"No need," I replied, opening the door to the backseat. She relinquished her bag, her fingers brushing mine as I took it from her, sending a hot sizzle of electricity up my arm.

Once we were in the car, after I got another eye roll from her when I held the door open, she glanced my way as I started the engine. "How far away is this place?"

"Hour and a half, give or take."

"I've heard it's a nice resort," she commented as I turned out of her driveway.

"I've heard the same. Can't say because I've never been there."

"Speaking of never being somewhere, where do you live on our road? You took me home that one time, but I've yet to see where your truck is parked."

I pointed as we passed by the driveway in question. "It's that house. Parking is in the back, so it wouldn't be obvious," I explained.

Quiet fell between us as I navigated from downtown Stolen Hearts Valley onto the highway that would take us north. Just when I was thinking perhaps quiet was best, if only because I could zone out and try to get my body's response to Jade under control, she spoke up.

"Okay, we need to make use of this time," she announced.

Sliding my eyes to hers, I arched a brow in question before facing forward to the highway again.

"You're bringing me to a wedding. This can't be just like a casual date. We have to know something about each other. When it comes to things like this, it's best if we just know the truth," she explained.

On the long list of things I hadn't considered when I'd impulsively asked Jade to come with me to this wedding, I could now add being quizzed.

"Have you done this before?" I asked.

Jade's husky laugh sounded too good and sent a sizzle down my spine. "Not specifically. When I was in college, I took every drama elective available just for fun, so I'm sure I can handle it."

"All right then, you tell me what we need to know."

"The basics. You know, from what we do to some details about our families. All I know about you is you work for Stolen Hearts Valley Emergency Response and at Stolen Hearts Lodge. You're friends with my brother, and you can handle a bar fight with no trouble."

"Well, that seems like plenty, don't you think?" I tossed that out there.

"Oh, definitely not. I need to know where you're from, and a little bit about your family so I can lie convincingly. Here, I'll start. I'm from Stolen Hearts Valley, grew up with Lucas. We've got a pretty typical family, two parents and two kids. I suppose the atypical part is our parents are still together, and they're actually still happy and in love. They also live in the same home where I grew up, which is only about five miles away from where I live. You know I bartend occasionally, but that's not a full-time job. I've been filling in more lately since Delilah left. For the last five years or so, I did full-time daycare for Lucas's daughter, Rylie. He and Valentina are a pretty new thing. Before Lucas met Valentina, he was a single dad. Rylie's mom died when she was only one year old."

My question rolled off my tongue because I was genuinely curious. "Before you started doing daycare full-time for Lucas, what were your plans?"

Jade let out a soft sigh. "I didn't have any clear plan. I got my degree in horticulture because I always loved gardening. I suppose my plan was to eventually start my own landscaping business. Working for Lucas didn't interfere because I needed to make some money. Our parents are great, but they aren't wealthy enough to pay for college. I'd planned all along to take some time to pay off my student loans and save some money before I tried to start a business. That's never cheap."

"Definitely not," I agreed. "I'm assuming I don't need to worry about any boyfriends." I slipped that one in, curious enough about her rumored no-dating stance to wonder what she was going to tell me.

Before she said a word, I could feel the tension suddenly hanging in the air. I flicked my eyes to the side, to see her jaw set in a tight line. She didn't exactly seem angry, but she was definitely not appreciating my question. After a moment, she replied, "Of course not. I wouldn't be here if I had a boyfriend. I don't date, and I intend for it to stay that way."

I filed that detail away, sliding it into one of the drawers in my brain that I might open again if I ever thought she'd tell me why. Because in all honesty, it was a damn shame for someone like Jade to swear off romance for her entire life. She was the kind of woman who didn't come along often.

She was steely and feisty with an earthy sensuality that called to me.

"While we're on the subject, what about you? Here I am, apparently your fake date, but it's not like you don't have your pick of women," she commented.

"The same could be said for you," I countered.

"Events happened, and I don't trust men. Unfortunately for me, I don't bat for the other team, although sometimes I wish I did," Jade replied.

I almost choked, letting out a surprised huff of a laugh. Jade winked and her lips curled in a slight smile. The temptation to hold her gaze was strong, and I had to force my eyes back to the road. We were going close to sixty miles per hour on a mountain highway, and it just wouldn't do for me to get lost in Jade's eyes.

"So, your turn," she added.

Keeping my gaze studiously forward, I offered a quick summary. "I grew up about an hour away from Stolen Hearts Valley. I enrolled in the Air Force and completed college while I was in the military. While I was overseas, my girlfriend, really the only serious one I've had, hooked up with my best friend's brother. She didn't ruin me, or anything like that. I won't lie and say it didn't sting my pride. Nobody likes to be made to look like a fool. But I figured it was for the best when all was said and done. Now, she can screw around on him. Back to my family. I grew up with two parents who actually loved each other. My dad passed away last summer after a heart attack."

Jade gasped. "I'm so sorry!"

Looking sideways, I saw she'd put her hand to her chest, and her eyes were wide. "Thank you. It sucked, and I miss him, but he died in his sleep, so I can't complain about that. I visit my mother every other month or so for a weekend."

"What brought you to Stolen Hearts Valley?"

"The job. Keeps me sane to stay outside. Jackson wants to start some small flights too, and I've got my pilots license.

That was an easy yes. Between the first responder crew and working at the lodge, it suits my personality."

"Any siblings?" Jade asked.

"Nope. Just me. I'd like to say I was spoiled, but not really. My dad was ex-military and pretty strict. We got by, but money was tight."

"Tell me about your best friend who's getting married. I need some details."

"I suppose that would help. It's my buddy, Dave. We went to high school together. He's a great guy. He's marrying his college sweetheart, Jenny."

"Got it. Now tell me about your ex."

"Dee."

"Dee who?"

"Dee Clark."

I felt Jade's attention on me, and I glanced to the side. She lifted a brow. "I need a little more history than that. Like how messy was it? That kind of thing." Jade circled her hand in the air.

I rolled my eyes, once again returning my focus to the road. The sun had started to slide down the sky, shifting from late afternoon into early evening and casting the mountains in a rosy gold glow.

"It wasn't a heartbreak. Dee and I dated a little bit in high school, and then reconnected one time when I was home for a visit. Honestly, she didn't break my heart. I felt foolish all right. I mean, who appreciates finding out his girlfriend is screwing around with their best friend's brother?"

"I certainly don't," Jade said, her tone firm.

"Right. So, it was just that. Nothing horrible. I cut things off right away so it didn't drag out."

"How long ago?"

"Last summer. That's when I finished my time with the Air Force. I found out when I got back."

"How'd you find out?"

"Damn, you're one with the questions."

Jade bopped me lightly on the shoulder with her fist. "Maybe I'm nosy, but it's so I have something to say if anybody asks me about it. People gossip, especially when they've had a few drinks. Maybe she didn't break your heart, but I'll be prepared to make her feel like an idiot."

"Is this personal for you or something?" I finally asked.

"Not me personally, but yes, it's personal. Lucas's ex screwed around on him. He didn't find out until after she died, but man, it was a bit of a mindfuck for him for a while."

I pointed out the obvious. "Lucas seems to be doing great now."

Her smile was wide. "Damn straight. He deserves a good woman, and Valentina is the best."

"It's obvious Lucas has it bad for her," I observed.

Jade nodded in satisfaction. "Okay, back to Dee. What do I need to know?"

"I came home from being overseas and found her in bed with Dave's brother. I broke up with her on the spot, and that was that. Honestly, I'm surprised they're still together. Lately, she's been texting me. I'm guessing she's fishing to try to get back together. I am *not* interested, and I'd rather not have to deal with it. Having you with me should help with that."

I could feel Jade shaking her head. "This is going to be fun. I get to really make her jealous."

I slid my eyes to hers. "You don't have to try that hard."

"If we don't make some effort, everyone's gonna know it's not a real thing."

I shook my head and left that alone. It wasn't real, and we needed to remember that. We managed to settle into an easy conversation for the remainder of the drive. When we pulled up to the picturesque resort, Jade let out a little sigh as I cut the engine.

"Oh wow, it's gorgeous here."

I followed her gaze. This winery and resort had become a

wedding destination in the last few years, or so Dave had told me. The sprawling hotel was nestled into a valley. The center of the hotel was three stories with two wings flanking it. The curved shape of the structure followed the lines of the mountain ridge behind it. The lawns surrounding it had a mix of hardwood trees scattered across the lush grass and offered an excellent view of a sparkling oval-shaped lake. Just now, the colors of the setting sun cast a watercolor shimmer of pink, purple, and gold across the surface.

I climbed out and rounded the truck to open Jade's door. I chuckled to myself when I got there to find her opening it.

"In case you didn't notice, I'm perfectly capable of opening a door for myself, Walker," she drawled as her eyes met mine.

She had started to slide off the seat with her cowboy boots resting on the running board. Maybe six inches separated us. In a flash, it felt as if the air hummed to life around us. That lust only Jade seemed to elicit whipped through me. I was tempted, so fucking tempted, to kiss her pretty mouth.

Chapter Seven

JADE

I stared up into Walker's silvery-gray gaze and tried to catch my breath. My lungs weren't doing the best job. I'd never experienced the concept of breathlessness and was irritated to find Walker had that effect on me just by getting a little too close.

I absorbed the way his eyes darkened like the summer sky when a storm was first building. My pulse skittered off wildly. I felt my hand curling around the door handle, as if that alone could anchor me and slow the sensations racing through my body.

"I'm aware you can open your own door, Jade." Walker's words came out slow and measured, the subtle twang in his voice making me shiver.

I had quite purposefully sworn off men. Until Walker, that hadn't been a problem. I hadn't even been tempted. Walker was turning out to be far more than I had bargained for. He was so purely masculine, and yet in such an understated way. I felt a low tug in my belly at his nearness.

The desire to yank him to me and feel his lips on mine

collided against the urge to run far and fast. Because I didn't know what to do with this feeling.

Just when I was thinking I couldn't take it anymore, his gaze broke from mine at the sound of someone calling his name. When he stepped back, I shimmied my hips down and jumped to the ground.

As it turned out, with the way Walker stood by the door, I landed right by his side. When the woman who called his name approached us, he dropped his hand from the door and slid his arm around my waist.

My breath hitched in my chest. I was flush against Walker's honed and strong body, and my body thought that was fan-fucking-tastic. My nipples practically stood up and cheered.

I presumed the woman approaching was Dee, primarily by the way her face fell when her eyes landed on me. She was pretty with chestnut brown hair that fell straight past her shoulders and bright blue eyes that locked onto me once she got close.

For just a beat, Dee's confident stride broke. I could practically feel her gather herself back together. She threw her shoulders back slightly and lifted her chin. With a flick of her manicured fingers, she brushed her hair off her shoulder as she came to a stop in front of us.

"Hi, Walker, how are you?"

Walker's hand slid down to rest on the curve of my hip. I was acutely aware of the heat of his touch. Here I thought this would be simple. I'd play the role of Walker's devoted girlfriend, and it would be fun. I didn't expect this much proximity to him. I didn't expect him to send me reeling inside with need spinning like hot sparks through me.

Willing my pulse to behave itself, I focused my attention on Dee and smiled politely. Walker was replying, "Doing quite well, Dee. And how are you?"

There was a tightness around her lips and eyes as her gaze flicked to me and back to Walker again. "I'm fine. It's been a rough few months, but then you know that. You seem to have neglected to let me know you were seeing someone," she said as she brought her gaze to me again.

I stepped a little closer to Walker. We were basically plastered to each other at this point. Sliding my arm around his waist, I smiled at Dee before looking up at him and not even faking the heat in my gaze.

Reluctantly, for real, I dragged my eyes away. "Hi, I'm Jade." I held out my free hand. Her hesitance to shake my hand was obvious, and I didn't even care. Her palm was cool, and her grip a little weak.

"I'm Dee," she said sharply. "Walker and I go way back."

"So I hear. I hope things are going well with your new boyfriend."

I felt Walker's fingers tighten on my hip and the subtle shake of a laugh when his ribs moved against my side. He didn't make a sound, though.

The lines around Dee's eyes tightened as her smile went from tense to brittle. Walker's hand squeezed my hip lightly again. I couldn't tell if that was because he was pleased with me teasing Dee, or warning me against it. Either way, my body sure liked the feel of it with a little zing spinning through me from his touch.

"Walker!" a man's voice called. "How ya doin', man?"

Walker shifted toward the source of the voice. A man with brown hair and a lanky stride was angling across the parking lot at an easy jog. Dee glanced in the same direction, annoyance flashing across her face, which she masked quickly.

"Hey, Dave," Walker said as the man reached us.

Dave pulled Walker into a back slapping hug before stepping away and glancing at me. "You must be Jade. So glad you could make it."

"You got it, this is Jade," Walker said.

His silver gaze collided with mine. A hot sizzle of heat raced through me from nothing more than the look in his eyes. This was getting out of hand. Flustered, I faced Dave, whom I knew to be Walker's best friend and the groom.

"I'm sorry we haven't had a chance to meet sooner. I wasn't about to miss your wedding, though," I said with a smile.

If Dave knew whether or not this was a fake date, he certainly didn't let on. He flashed a grin. "Thrilled you could make it," he told Dee, coolness entering his gaze. "Steve is looking for you. Are you all set with your room?"

Dee smiled tightly. "Of course we are. We checked in last night."

"Oh, that's right. Jenny and I didn't see you yesterday, so I spaced that y'all checked in early," Dave replied.

"Well, I should go. I've got a few things to take care of before the rehearsal dinner," Dee said. "Nice to meet you, Jade." I was pretty sure it about killed her to be polite, but she managed it. Her eyes landed on Walker. "I sure hope we get a chance to talk."

"So nice to meet you," I said, injecting a cheery tone in my voice, which really wasn't all that hard.

Meanwhile, Walker simply inclined his head. "Good to see you, Dee."

Dave waggled his eyebrows at Walker when Dee walked away, her heels clicking in a staccato rhythm on the pavement as she crossed the parking lot. Only after she disappeared inside the hotel did Dave roll his eyes, hard. "Damn, I wish like hell she wasn't here. Hope she's not too much of a pain in your ass."

Walker chuckled and shrugged. "She's not. That's why I've got Jade here with me."

Dave glanced at me. "Walker tells me you're up for the task of being his girlfriend for the weekend." He offered this with a sly smile.

"I sure am. Can you clarify something for me, though?" I asked, glancing between them. Walker and I had covered a number of topics on the drive here, but I hadn't clarified one detail.

"Ask away," Walker drawled while Dave nodded.

"How are things with Dee and your brother?" I asked Dave.

"Ugh. They're not too happy with each other, and I don't know why they're still sticking it out. He's no idiot. He knows she's been barking back up another tree," Dave replied with a shake of his head.

I snorted a laugh. "Is the tree Walker?"

Walker rolled his eyes. "Tree? Do I look like a tree?"

Dave shrugged nonchalantly. "Nope, but you catch my drift. She's trying to piss on you to make it clear she owns you. She does *not* fucking get that she already fucked around on you, and she can't pull that shit again. I told my mom I'd rather not even have Steve here. We've never really gotten along. It's a big wedding, though, and you know my family." He addressed that last comment to Walker.

"Oh, yeah, I do. Don't worry. I got this," Walker said. I got another little squeeze on my hip with that comment. If Walker kept up with being all touchy-feely, I was going to have a problem.

Another car rolled into the parking lot with a man in the driver's seat waving toward Dave. "Catch you later. Gotta do more greetings. You'll be at the rehearsal dinner tonight, right?"

"I wasn't under the impression I was allowed to ignore it. I *am* the best man after all," Walker returned.

Dave winked. "Yeah, but you never were one to toe the line if you didn't feel like it. I'll see y'all there. Just text me if you need anything."

Dave jogged off, and Walker pulled our bags out of the back of his truck. When I attempted to help, he gave me a look.

"What's that look for?" I asked.

"I know you can carry your bag, but so can I. Come on, Jade."

"Won't it look better if I carry my bag and we hold hands?"

One dark brow rose in a slash and a laugh rumbled in his chest. "You are *good*. All right. Carry your bag."

He handed it over. Once I had a grip on it, he reached for my free hand. His large palm engulfed mine. As we strolled across the parking lot, I felt a pair of eyes on me and found Dee watching us from the porch that ran the length of the center part of the hotel. Walker didn't appear to notice.

Within a few minutes, we'd passed through the understated and elegant lobby area and checked in. Walker had declined any assistance getting our bags in our room. My hand was still warm in his as we walked down the hallway to our room on the third floor.

When we stepped in the room, I wandered around. It was, of course, lovely. The room was decorated in soft pastels. The walls were painted dove gray with touches of lavender in the trim, and a fluffy gray down quilt on the bed. With it being late spring, the days were already getting hot and humid, although I expected the nights to be cool here in the mountains just like they were in Stolen Hearts Valley.

Walker had already explained we'd be sharing a room. I understood why. It would seem out of place if we had separate rooms. He had assured me he'd called ahead and tactfully requested a room with a foldout sofa bed.

After we set our bags down, I stared out the windows, marveling that we had our own private balcony with a glorious view of the lake. The sun was setting, leaving the sky splashed with fading colors and casting the mountain ridge in shadow.

"We have a small problem," Walker said, his voice drawing my attention away from the view.

Turning back, I asked, "What's that?"

His intent silver gaze held mine for a beat before he looked sideways at the bed. I somehow doubted the bed appreciated his eyes as much as I did.

"What's wrong with the bed?" I asked.

Walker's eyes caught mine again, and it felt as if lightning flashed between us. "There's only one. We were supposed to get a room with a foldout sofa," he explained.

"Oh. I'm sure it will be fine," I said hurriedly.

Walker began to pull his phone out of his pocket, but I shook my head. "Walker, you heard the woman at the reception desk. The hotel is booked through the weekend for this wedding and another one a few days later. If you think no one will notice if we try to switch rooms when we probably have one of the best here, you're crazy. Let's just deal with it. I'll sleep on the floor."

My words, which sounded rational enough, only added to the tension spinning inside me. My inconvenient reaction to Walker was muddling my thinking.

"Jesus, Jade. You can't sleep on the floor. I'll sleep on the floor."

We turned together to the bed. It was a massive bed, practically big enough for me to run laps around it.

I knew the second Walker looked at me. I could feel the heat of his gaze on me. Glancing over, I smiled encouragingly. "Really, it'll be fine. I'd hate for you to sleep on the floor."

"Don't take this the wrong way, Jade, but I promised Lucas that this was a totally platonic thing. I don't want there to be any confusion about that."

I narrowed my eyes. "Oh, for God's sake. This isn't some kind of little sister thing where you have to answer to my brother. We're adults. There're about thirty pillows on the bed. We'll just stack some in between us."

With a huff, I crossed my arms, staring Walker down.

Chapter Eight

WALKER

Laughter, music, and the murmur of voices surrounded me. I lifted my scotch and took a quick swallow, savoring the smooth flavor.

"So," Dave began, "you didn't mention how gorgeous your date was."

Sliding my gaze sideways, I shrugged. "Does that matter?"

Dave's gaze met mine, a gleam in his eyes. "Not particularly. Except for the fact you can't keep your eyes off Jade if she's anywhere nearby. You sure she's not the real deal?"

Don't I fucking wish?

I kept that thought to myself. "She's a friend. Actually, she's more of an acquaintance. Her brother is a friend. He's on the first responder crew with me. Totally good guy. You'd like him. Anyway, Jade—" I gestured in her direction, which gave me an excuse to look at her. Sweet hell, she looked amazing. She was wearing some sort of gauzy wrap dress in purple that made her eyes pop. Her dark hair fell in a cascade around her shoulders, the lights a shimmering reflection in her locks.

"You were saying?" Dave drawled. When I brought my gaze back to him, he winked.

"I helped her out in a pinch one night where she works at a local bar. After all was said and done, she commented that she owed me a favor. With Dee trying to call and text, I figured it was best if I didn't come alone, so I took her up on it. That's all there is to it."

I wasn't about to admit out loud that I'd thought maybe I could use this weekend with her as a chance to burn the fire kindling between us to ashes. I'd been trying to forget I'd ever even considered that.

Dave gave me a long look before chuckling. "Right. Go ahead and tell yourself that. All I know is I've never seen you look at a woman like that."

"Well, she *is* beautiful."

"True. Maybe she'll be more than your fake date."

Lifting my scotch, I drained the last of it. I could've argued the point with Dave, but that might've given me away. No matter how much I tried to ignore it, I knew I was drawn to Jade.

Dave's fiancée, Jenny, slipped into a chair beside him. "Hey, babe," she said with a slightly tipsy grin.

Dave's gaze softened, and he lifted a hand to smooth her hair away from her forehead, his touch gentle. Here was the guy who never took any dates seriously, the guy who got skittish if a girl wanted to spend the night. Dave had never been the worst sort of player. He wasn't like that. He just liked to keep things "clear" as he put it. He fell so hard and fast for Jenny, I was still giving him hell about it. Case in point: he leaned over to kiss the side of her neck and whispered something in her ear.

"Jenny, you own that man. He takes whipped to new levels," I observed.

Jenny's brown eyes twinkled when she smiled. "It's a two-way street."

Dave was entirely unperturbed by my teasing and slid an

arm around her shoulders before pressing a kiss to her temple. "I don't care. I might as well be whipped. We *are* getting married. Better make it worth it."

I grinned. "You are, and I am truly happy for the two of you. You better treat him right now, Jenny."

Jenny angled her head to the side as she smiled over at me. "As if I would do anything else." She shifted gears smoothly. "So, Jade is nice. I hear Dave and I are the only two privy to your true situation."

Glancing from Dave to Jenny, I shrugged. "You are, and I'd like to keep it that way."

Jenny's smile was cheeky in return. "Oh, I love keeping a good secret. This one's worthy. Dee's an idiot. She cheated on you before, and now she's tired of Steve, so she wants a change. I suggested she just cheat on him."

Dave sputtered from the sip of his drink he'd just taken. "Did you really?"

"Oh, hell yes. She knows what I think of her. I have no reason to play nice. This is *my* wedding. She knows if she dares to make a scene, I'll make her regret it," Jenny said firmly.

Dave said something, and then they were kissing again.

I stood to go get a refill of my drink. In my conversation with Dave and Jenny, I'd lost sight of Jade. My eyes landed on her over at the bar. Some guy I didn't recognize was talking to her and staring down her cleavage. I felt my metaphorical hackles rise up. This was a new one for me. I hadn't had many girlfriends, simply because life hadn't offered much time or space for it. I sure as hell had never experienced jealousy or possessiveness. Nothing like what I felt when I saw that guy trying to get a nice view down Jade's dress.

As I approached, I heard the man comment to Jade, "I'll get this one for you, sweetheart."

Jade's tart reply was swift. "I'm not your sweetheart, and no thank you."

The guy was idiot enough to persist. "Oh, come on, it's just a drink." He said something to the bartender, who didn't seem aware of Jade's irritation.

I strode toward Jade, not even bothering to be polite and stepping between her and the guy. He was close to my height, but not quite. "Hey, darlin'," I said, sliding my arm around her waist.

When I looked down into her eyes, I was startled to see fear flickering in their depths. Her breath was shallow, and her skin was a little pale. Although I didn't know what was going on, I was instantly pissed off at the idiot.

"Excuse me," he interjected. "I was just buying this lovely lady a drink."

"And this lovely lady just told you she didn't want a drink," Jade said sharply.

Glancing at him, I sensed he was trying to play it cool. He hadn't stepped back, despite me crowding in between them. Fuck that. Narrowing my eyes, I asked, "You always insist on buying drinks for women to tell you they don't fucking want them? Let me guess, you don't know how to take no for an answer."

"Oh, for fuck's sake," he muttered. "It's just a drink."

"She told you she didn't want a drink. She's also here with me," I said flatly before averting my gaze.

"Maybe you should've made that more obvious," he sneered.

I whipped my head back in his direction. "She doesn't need a keeper."

Jade was still tense, a subtle tremor running through her. Casting about in my mind, I couldn't put my finger on what was unsettling her so. I'd seen Jade handle assholes at Lost Deer Bar on more than one occasion. But something about this situation wasn't comfortable for her, and I didn't like seeing her like this.

"Do you want to go back to our room?" I asked, leaning down to whisper in her ear.

She shook her head. "No, let's just get a table."

Keeping my arm around her waist, I guided her away from the bar. Only to have that asshole's voice follow us. "You might as well take the drink. I already ordered it, so I have to pay for it."

"I'm not taking his drink," Jade whispered with her teeth clenching.

Glancing over my shoulder, I shook my head. "She doesn't want your drink. Drop it."

Just when I thought he was actually going to persist, another woman approached the bar, and his attention was redirected.

With Jade's warm, albeit tense, body pressed against my side, we walked across the restaurant. I spied a table in the corner and snagged it. Pulling out a chair, I waited until Jade was seated before sitting down across from her. Her expression had softened, and that hint of fear I'd seen was replaced with annoyance.

"I hate guys like him. One thing that's nice about being a bartender is I can make sure idiots like him don't take advantage of anyone," she said. She must've seen the confusion on my face. "It may sound paranoid, but it's not that unusual for guys to buy drinks to spike them first with one of those date rape drugs before handing it over because they can't get laid on their own merits."

It's not as if I hadn't heard of that before, but still, it was shocking to consider. After a beat, I said, "I've heard about that. Can't say I like having to think about it much. I do appreciate the way you frame it. On their merits."

"Well, it's true. They actually include that in our training at Lost Deer Bar. I'm just a fill-in, and I still had to get the training on that. It's kind of depressing, but it's a thing."

"I suppose so." Pausing, I reached for her hand, only to find it cold. I gave it a gentle squeeze. "Thanks for coming to the rehearsal dinner."

Jade smiled and slid her hand out from under mine

before drumming her fingertips on the table. She'd painted her nails a deep purple to match her wrap dress. My eyes were drawn to the bright color. I had to force my gaze to return to her face and not linger on the sweet curves of her body on the way up.

A waiter stopped by our table. "Y'all need anything?" he asked politely.

I gestured for Jade to answer. "I'll take one of those frozen strawberry margaritas. I saw someone with one earlier, and it looked amazing," she said.

"You got it." He tapped something in the small computer tablet he held in his hand before his eyes bounced to me.

"I'll take a scotch on the rocks."

"Be right back," he said before striding quickly to the bar.

"Dave and Jenny are a sweet couple," Jade commented when we were alone again.

I grinned. "I'll have to tell Dave you described him as sweet. He'll appreciate that."

Jade let out a throaty laugh. The sound sent a hot jolt of lust through me. I was reconsidering whether a bolster of pillows between us on the bed would be sufficient. I just might need a cold shower and to sleep on the floor. Even though I'd originally thought some time with Jade would be a good way to burn through my attraction to her, that didn't seem like a wise plan. There was too much power to it, and Jade was too damn tempting.

"In all seriousness," I added, looping back to Jade's comment. "They're a great couple. I'm happy for Dave and Jenny."

"Your ex approached me in the ladies room." Jade's eyes held a sly gleam.

"Oh God. You're kidding me, right?"

She shook her head slowly. "God, no. I overheard her talking to some other woman whose name I didn't catch. I was in the stall, and they didn't know I was there. Apparently, she thinks Dave's brother might be cheating on her. She was all upset about it. And, she's pissy that you brought a date. I guess she thought she might have a chance to talk to you. So when I came out of the stall, I told her if she hadn't screwed around on you in the first place, maybe she wouldn't be in this position."

I threw my head back with a laugh. "Damn, Jade. You must be driving Dee crazy. All I needed was a little help getting her to leave me alone. You've more than done your job with that."

"Oh, I don't think she's going to give up. She told me she knew you still loved her deep down inside."

"That's ridiculous. I don't think I ever said the word love. We dated for a bit, and I went overseas. Yes, we stayed in touch. Yes, I thought we were exclusive. But for God's sake, I don't think many people can understand the concept of love when they're that young and that far apart. Myself included."

A slow grin unfurled on Jade's face. "I thought she was full of it."

Our waiter returned at that moment with our drinks. While he was serving us, Dave and Jenny meandered over to join us. Conversation moved on, and Jade seemed to relax again. I couldn't help but wonder about the flicker of tension and fear I'd seen in her eyes when that guy tried to buy her a drink.

Chapter Nine

JADE

When I opened my eyes, nothing more than a glimmer of light was coming through the sheer gray curtains. My mind was hazy with sleep, and I felt strangely warm and safe. As I came more fully awake, for a flash I was confused and almost scrambled out of bed. But then, I remembered where I was. I closed my eyes tightly again.

I was at the wedding with Walker, and we'd piled pillows between us last night. I was surprised I even remembered that because I'd let myself get tipsy, something I rarely did.

The pillows hadn't done their job. I was pressed against Walker's side where he lay on his back. His muscled arm was curled around me, his palm cupping my bottom. I even had one of my legs thrown over his. I was as closely tangled up with him as I could possibly be.

Once my sleep muddled confusion cleared, I considered my situation. I should've wanted to get out of the bed as fast as possible. But I didn't want to move. At all. It felt so good to be curled against Walker and held tight.

Opening my eyes for the second time, I let my gaze examine him in the almost darkness. Walker's profile was strong and clean. With his dark brow, the elegant angle of his cheekbone and the square edge of his jaw, his lips were a sensual tease in contrast. He had full lips that curled slightly at the corners even in sleep. He wasn't the cheeriest guy by nature, so it was almost funny, as if his mouth was attempting to debate the point with his tendency to be all broody and quiet. Broody wasn't quite fair. He was more quiet and reserved, as if he only let some people beyond that guard. I wanted to be lucky enough to see behind that exterior. I'd seen hints of it last night in his easy banter with his friends.

Walker's breathing suddenly changed in rhythm and I tensed, thinking I should move away. After a beat, he opened his eyes, immediately rolling his head to the side. His silver gaze met mine.

"So much for those pillows," he said, his voice, softened by sleep, curled around me. His soft drawl did funny things to my belly.

I never thought a man's voice could get to me. I'd always appreciated a Southern accent, but more in an objective way. With Walker, it was downright sexy, bordering on naughty, every time he spoke. And, the way his voice made me feel was the opposite of objective. It sent sparks of heat skittering through me, which left me tingling from head to toe.

"I guess," I finally managed.

My body had other ideas, but I managed to force myself to move away. I'd fallen asleep in a pair of lightweight cotton pants and a T-shirt. My feet swung to the floor, and I eyed my painted toenails, acutely aware that my nipples were tight and achy.

Considering the state of my body, I was certain Walker had felt them pressed against his side. Of all the things I hadn't thought through when I offered to do this, I had grossly underestimated the intensity of my response to him.

I did what I usually did when I was uncomfortable. I reasoned I could ignore it, and it would go away. Standing, I rounded the foot of the bed. "Mind if I use the shower first?"

"Nah, go right ahead."

I made the mistake of glancing in his direction. It was then I noticed the distinct outline of his arousal under the sheets. I also remembered him climbing into bed in his fitted boxer briefs, black of course. My slightly tipsy brain had admired the sight of his tight ass.

Heat blasted through me, and I looked away abruptly, practically running into the bathroom. I started my shower cold, in an effort to douse the arousal burning me up inside. Once I had effectively cooled off, I turned the hot water on and finished my shower. It was only after I stepped out that I realized I didn't bring any clothes in here. Flustered, I pulled back on what I'd slept in and stepped out to find Walker gone.

I was unaccountably relieved. Glancing at the clock on the nightstand beside the bed, I mentally noted we had an hour and a half before we needed to be downstairs for a breakfast for the wedding party and their respective dates.

That meant I needed to be in my wedding finery a few minutes before that time was up. Uncertain exactly when Walker would return, I scurried over to the closet and pulled out my dress. I was wearing a silk dress that had a soft fit. It was a lavender shade, so it matched my nails.

Snagging my clothes and what little I used as far as makeup and hair products went, I hurried back into the bathroom. Not much later, and I was almost ready. Except for one small detail. I needed help zipping up my dress.

"Fuck," I muttered to myself just as I heard the door to our room open and close.

"I've got coffee," Walker's voice called.

"I'll be out in a minute," I called in return.

I tried to fiddle my zipper up, but there was no way around it. I was going to need Walker's help with it. Considering I'd woken up tangled like a vine around him, I figured him zipping my dress would be no big deal.

I added a dash of powder on my skin to be prepared for the humidity that was to come, and a hint of hair cream I used to keep my hair from getting frizzy in the heat. It was mostly straight, but it could frizz when it was too sticky out. Pink lip gloss and smoky eyeliner finished it off. I wasn't much for makeup, but I did like to look good when the occasion called for it. This was a wedding, and I happened to be the date of the best man, so I needed to put on a good show. Not to mention that I did genuinely want to make Dee jealous. Not of me per se... Okay, I wanted her to be jealous of me. Which was crazy thinking. This inconvenient attraction was stirring up all kinds of irrational feelings.

Stepping out of the bathroom, I found Walker already dressed. His hair was damp, clearly from a shower. "Okay, how'd you pull that off?" I asked, resting a hand on my hip as I gave him a once-over.

Walker in a suit was downright dangerous. I was going to need a fan. Heat licked over my skin and my pulse took off. He wore a charcoal gray suit, which merely served to set off his silver smoke eyes. At the moment, his crisp white shirt was open at the collar. He glanced over, casting me a quick smile.

"I figured you might need some time to get ready. Dave had already told me they had a suite set aside for any of the men whose partners might be tying up the hotel bathrooms. I snagged a shower and a shave. It's early enough that no one else was there yet."

He shrugged out of his jacket, and my eyes landed on the flex of his shoulders as he moved. He draped his jacket over the back of a chair beside the dresser. Rolling up his shirt sleeves, I was then treated to the sight of one of his muscular forearms flexing as he lifted a cup of coffee and took a swallow. "Got one for you," he said, nodding to the desk where he'd set another cup of coffee.

This was what I'd been reduced to—a woman in thrall of a forearm flex and the almost drool-worthy temptation of the V of skin showing at the top of his white shirt. I wanted to lick him. Lick him! Dear God. I needed to get a grip.

Stepping closer, I lifted the coffee cup.

"I guessed you preferred your coffee with cream," he said, his gaze sweeping up and down my body.

"You guessed right." I took a sip, closing my eyes and savoring the flavor. Opening them, I said, "Thank you. This is some seriously good coffee."

Walker flashed a smile. "Can't take credit for it, but it is delicious." He paused, his eyes assessing. "You look beautiful."

I flushed all over again. It shouldn't matter what Walker thought of how I looked, but it did. I didn't sense Walker was a man to hand out compliments easily. I wanted him to notice me just as much as I didn't want to want him to notice me. Talk about conflicted.

"I actually need help with my zipper. I was hoping you wouldn't mind."

He set his coffee down on the dresser. "Of course not."

I turned, lifting my hair and spinning it around my hand as I pulled it over my shoulder. "There you go. I'm sure you can handle a zipper and don't need instructions, right?" I teased in an attempt to keep myself distracted.

Walker's responding chuckle sent a prickle chasing over my skin. He rested one hand on the curve of my hip. With the other, he caught the zipper pull and drew it up slowly. One of his knuckles brushed lightly against my spine on the ascent.

That subtle touch and the soft sound of the zipper felt like a string pulling tighter and tighter inside, spinning me full of need. I was practically breathless by the time he reached the top. No more than a few seconds could've passed. And yet, time didn't particularly seem to matter when it came to the way I felt around Walker.

I swallowed and attempted to take a breath, getting no more than a little sip of air in my lungs. That did absolutely nothing to quell my racing heartbeat and the butterflies amassing in my belly.

"There."

A single word, spoken in Walker's gruff voice, reverberated through my body. I was feeling so off-kilter with the way this chemistry kept burgeoning between us that I suddenly wanted to take control of it. Maybe then, it would dissipate.

Whether I was alone in this or not, I knew I recognized the answering flare of desire and the heat banked in his gaze. Electricity sizzled between us.

Galvanized, whether by my decision to take control of the driving force inside of me or something else, I stepped closer and lifted my hand, letting it fall lightly on his chest. Through the thin cotton shirt, I could feel him as I slid my palm across the surface. His chest was all hard, muscled planes, just as I'd expected. His eyes widened slightly.

"Here's the thing, Walker. Inconvenient though it may be, I want you. Speak now or forever hold your peace if you'd rather me not kiss you right this second," I whispered.

A glint entered his gaze, but he stayed silent. Sliding my hand up to cup his nape, I gave a light tug, and he met me halfway. I liked to feel in control. I *needed* to feel in control in situations like this. Or so I thought. A sense of relief I didn't want to consider washed through me when he didn't try to go all manly and alpha on me.

I brushed my lips against his, once and then twice, before arching up further. Only then did Walker assume control. Angling his head to the side, he murmured something softly against my lips. I sighed against his mouth, and his tongue swept in.

One of his arms, strong and sure, slid around my waist, cupping the edge of my hip and teasing over the curve of my bottom as he pulled me against him. Oh hell. Being plastered against Walker and feeling the beat of his heart while mine went wild in my chest made me temporarily lose my mind.

The tease of his tongue wasn't overwhelming, just a stroke against mine and then another before he drew back and brushed his lips across mine again. He caught my bottom lip lightly in his teeth as he straightened.

We stared at each other, the air around us alive with a humming, nearly electric desire.

"I suppose I can speak now," he murmured in a gruff whisper.

I swallowed and licked my lips before nodding. "Yes."

Walker's smoky gaze searched mine as I tried and completely failed to get my pulse to slow down. The silence felt loaded and heavy, crowded with my thoughts and his. I liked to think I could read people pretty well. And yet, the brutal betrayal of one friend had thoroughly thrown that into doubt forever.

The circle of people I trusted was small. My family, and a tight group of friends. That was about it. Which made it all the more puzzling why I felt an intrinsic urge to trust Walker. I managed a shaky breath, unable to tear my eyes away from his.

"Well, now, I'd be lying if I said I didn't want you to kiss me. But, I'd also be lying if I said you didn't surprise the hell out of me with that," he drawled.

I licked my lips again and managed enough air to give myself a hint of fortitude. I tried my best to seem nonchalant and lifted a shoulder in a small shrug. "I can't help it that you look good enough to eat. Don't even try to tell me you're not aware that plenty of women wouldn't mind kissing you."

Walker's gaze was inscrutable. "That wasn't quite my point. But if that's the direction we're gonna go, I guess I could point out that I doubt it's escaped your notice that plenty of men can't keep their eyes off you," he said bluntly.

We stared at each other, the air practically vibrating between us.

"Shall we leave it at that?" he asked as he took a step back, beginning to carefully unroll his sleeves and button the cuffs.

"What do you mean?"

I could hardly believe it but a shaft of disappointment pierced me when he stepped away. I didn't like thinking about how much I enjoyed being held by Walker.

"I mean, are we gonna leave it at just that kiss? We do have a wedding and two more nights here," he replied.

My body felt as if lightning was pinging around inside of it. The need Walker kindled within me was unfamiliar. Frankly, it was something I didn't expect to ever have to deal with. I had made a decision that I wasn't going to date for very good reasons. It had been a decision that had been easy to make and easy to keep. So far.

Because no one tempted me, not even a little. Until now. The temptation of Walker was downright overwhelming. My senses were rioting, and I thought it would be worth making an exception. Not a relationship, but maybe an eyes-open-wide fling.

With my heart hammering away, I lifted my chin slightly. "Maybe not. What do you think?"

"I think you're complicated, and a helluva lot more than I bargained for. I also think your brother would kick my fucking ass," Walker said flatly.

Anger ran through me in a hot sizzle. Narrowing my eyes, I rested a hand on my hip. "Don't you dare fucking tell me that my brother has any say. What happens between us, or me and anyone for that matter, is none of his goddamned business."

A glint entered Walker's gaze, his lips curling at one corner as he eyed me before turning away to snag his suit jacket off the back of the chair and shrug into it. Dear God.

He was too much. His shoulders filled out his jacket quite nicely.

The charcoal gray against the crisp white of his shirt and his deep bronze skin sent my belly into a somersault and my pulse revving.

"I wasn't implying this was any of your brother's business," he finally said. "I was just making an observation."

Whether it made a lick of sense or not, somehow having Walker voice his concern about Lucas's possible opinion galvanized me. On the heels of a ragged breath, I said, "Well, good then. We have two nights. That's it. Let's make the most of them."

Chapter Ten

WALKER

I watched as my oldest friend said "I do" without even the slightest hesitation. If you'd asked me before Dave met Jenny if he'd ever settle down, or even entertain the idea of happily ever after, I would've laughed good and hard. He would've laughed right along with me.

Yet, I didn't doubt for one second just how deeply he'd fallen in love. Dave was a loyal man, and his commitment would never waver.

I found it hard to consider the possibility that I could fall for someone the way he had. Although the fact he actually had made me wonder. I'd reached a point with women where I didn't even think attraction meant all that much.

Although Dee hadn't broken my heart, she'd certainly contributed to my natural tendency to be cynical. My parents had loved each other, and my mother still hadn't recovered from my dad passing away. That was something I didn't want to experience. Between that and a few years in the military where I'd gotten up close and personal with how fast life could be snatched away, I figured I was better off alone.

All that said, meaningless sex was tiring. However, the way I felt with Jade was weighted with meaning. Jade lit a fire in me. I didn't think the fire burning for her was going to be extinguished by ignoring her. Especially not now, after she'd gone and kissed me. Hell, it had been bad enough last night when I woke up with her curled up against me.

My attention was on Jade when a flower landed on my shoulder as Jenny tossed her bouquet into the crowd. Lifting the white rose, I spun it in my fingers. Dave's laugh drew my eyes sideways. I was standing beside him at the top of the steps where he'd stepped back to give his new wife space for this ritual.

"Good luck," he said, clapping me on the shoulder.

I looked into the crowd to see one of the bridesmaids clutching the remainder of the flower bouquet in her hands. "Whoever caught it is up next. Or something like that, if you believe in this kind of thing," I said, my tone dry as chalk.

Dave chuckled. "You believe I love Jenny?"

Although there was laughter around us and a giddy sense of celebration, the moment felt suddenly serious. Holding Dave's gaze, I nodded. Because I wasn't going to lie to him. "I know you love her," I said quietly. "And I don't doubt y'all will be happy. I've threatened to kick her ass if she dares to break your heart."

Dave's lips quirked in a smile, although his eyes remained somber. "I do love her. And if you believe that, then whether you want to admit it or not, you believe in that romantic stuff. Go find Jade," he said with a nudge on my shoulder. "You still have a few toasts to give. First, we've got to get to the reception, and you need your date with you for that."

"Wait, did I miss something? Isn't the reception here at the hotel?"

Dave chuckled. "Absolutely. It's upstairs. But Jenny wanted a drive in the car, so she's going to get it."

I watched as Dave threaded his way through the crowd,

where his bride had already gotten swept up in the chatter of well wishes from the wedding guests. Letting my eyes scan the group, it only took a second for me to find Jade. Even from a distance, she was a magnet for my eyes. More than that, she was a magnet for me. She stood beside Jenny's sister, smiling politely, and nodding at something she said. Jade had carried off our dating subterfuge with aplomb.

Without even thinking, I was moving toward her. I hadn't forgotten her words this morning. *We have two nights.*

I wasn't sure if her words were a promise or a dare. I wasn't about to back down from the dare, and I always kept my promises.

Someone caught my elbow, gripping just tightly enough that I couldn't ignore it. Stopping in the crush of bodies, I noticed Dee over my shoulder. Her features were tight, and her smile brittle. I was honestly puzzled at what I had ever seen in her. Dee was a pretty woman. I was relieved I'd never fancied myself in love with her.

Being Dave's best man, I'd been fully prepared for Dave's brother to stand up as one of the groomsmen, but Dave had wanted a best man and nothing more. Funny that his brother had seen fit to apologize to me late last night after the reception dinner. Steve was just as much of an ass as he'd always been, but I'd simply shrugged and accepted the apology.

When I met Dee's eyes, I arched a brow.

"I was hoping we could talk," she said hurriedly.

Cocking my head to the side, I replied, "Dee, we have nothing to talk about. Like I told you already, I wish you the best."

I meant every word I said, which was a relief. I knew my tendency to be blunt and straightforward wasn't always appreciated. Why Dee wanted to attempt to have any kind of conversation in the middle of this crowd was beyond me. But then, I presumed she was aware she wasn't going to get an opportunity to be alone with me. I'd brushed her off via text and phone for the last month or more every time she reached out.

Dee bit her lip and looked away, before turning back, a crease forming between her brows. "You could've told me you were involved with someone," she said accusingly. As if she had any right to have any fucking opinion on the matter.

I was, frankly, confused by this. "Dee, no offense, but why would I keep you up to date on my love life? If you recall, you started another relationship with my best friend's brother while I was overseas. I'm not going to make it seem like we were truly, madly, deeply or anything like that—"

Dee's lips tightened in a line right before she interjected. "Make no mistake, Walker, I'm well aware that we were not 'truly, madly, deeply,' as you put it." She finished that off with air quotes. Dear God, I loathed drama.

"Right. Anyway. No hearts were broken. I wish you nothing but happiness." I couldn't believe that rolled out of my mouth, but I was feeling a tad sarcastic, to say the least.

Dee took a deep breath and let it out with a gusty sigh. "It's obvious Jade means far more to you than I ever did."

My annoyance bubbled over. "Dee, why the hell are you trying to talk to me about anything?" I shifted my shoulders slightly, feeling restless. I couldn't put a finger on what I felt toward Jade. However, I wasn't going to argue with myself about the depth of my instinctive response to her.

With Jade, it felt as if lightning was striking in the air around us whenever we got too close. My reaction to her was primitive and raw. Just the act of helping her with the zipper on her dress and that subtle point of contact where my knuckle rubbed against her skin was like tires burning on pavement. Just now, I could feel the visceral heat of the burn simply from recalling it.

With a sharp nod in Dee's direction and unwilling to entertain her wish to talk to me any longer, I dislodged her hand on my elbow. "Enjoy the rest of the wedding."

If anyone around us noticed the tension on Dee's

features, I didn't care. I made my way through the jostle of bodies as people began moving toward the steps where the reception was being held. When I got closer to Jade, I noticed there was another man talking with her. He was staring down at her cleavage, and I didn't appreciate the look in his eyes.

A fierce streak of possessiveness raced through me. I stepped to her side, sliding my hand around her waist and letting it rest on the soft curve of her hip. "Hey there," I murmured as I bent low and pressed a kiss to the side of her neck.

When I lifted my eyes, I met hers and didn't miss the sudden flash in them. Although we were ostensibly pretending we were together, I'd just gone a step further than we had taken it thus far in public by kissing her on the neck like that. I didn't care.

I felt her tremble slightly and watched the pink crest high on her cheeks. A subtle buzz of satisfaction ran through me. If I was going to be a slave to my reaction to her, I wouldn't mind knowing that maybe, just maybe, she might be as affected by me.

"Hey yourself." Her reply was husky, and I wanted to kiss her properly. That might be taking things too far just now.

Instead I straightened and looked at the man beside her. "I don't think we've met. Walker Hudson," I said with a nod, keeping my tone level.

The man's eyes bounced between us, his gaze cooling as he took the measure of the moment. He nodded in return. "Clyde Phelps. You're the best man, right?" At my nod, he continued, "Are you as surprised as I was to see Dave fall so hard and fast?" he asked conversationally.

Considering that I didn't know this man, and knew Dave really well, I knew they weren't close. Be that as it may, Dave's days of being a player weren't exactly a secret. I simply smiled. "Perhaps at first. But then I met Jenny. Dave is nothing if not loyal. He was guaranteed to fall hard, and

I'm nothing but thrilled for him. Nice to meet you. We'll be going because we need to get into the reception."

I didn't wait for Clyde's reply. He called after us, "Nice to meet you, Jade. Y'all enjoy the rest of your weekend."

With my arm firmly around Jade's waist, I steered her through the crowd as we made our way into the reception. I had to admit, Jade had thoroughly dissuaded me from the idea that I had control of this situation. If she hadn't gone and kissed me this morning, I might've been able to live within that illusion.

As we crested the top of the stairs, Jade murmured, "Well, I must admit you're good at marking your territory."

"Excuse me?"

We stopped in the hallway where it was quieter, the voices muted from the large event room nearby where the reception was being held and the crowd was filtering in.

Jade moved slightly, not stepping away from where my arm was wrapped around her waist, but shifting to face me better. Her dark hair fell to the side, and she brushed it over her shoulder. "Mark your territory. You know, showing up when that guy was being nothing more than polite to me. I swear, men can be just like dogs. Actually, that's not fair. I adore dogs."

I couldn't help it. I burst out laughing. "I love dogs too, so I don't mind being compared to them."

Jade rolled her eyes.

"You did say we needed to put on a good act. Also, you kissed me this morning, so you started it."

"Is that what I did?" she murmured, her cheeks flushing a deeper shade of pink.

I didn't know why I said what I said next. Maybe it was all this talk about weddings and love. Maybe it was watching my best friend get married. Maybe it was Dave's passing comment that I must believe in love if I believed he loved Jenny. Maybe it was because my brain was addled by the hum of desire sizzling through me whenever I was near Jade.

Maybe it was my ex-girlfriend's observation that I seemed to have a lot more with Jade than I'd ever had with her. I didn't think I would ever know what prompted my next comment.

Yet, the curiosity had been simmering under the surface ever since I heard the rumors that Jade didn't ever date and was open about her intention never to do so. I wasn't usually curious like this. But, there were a lot of things I wasn't *usually* like when it came to Jade.

"Rumor has it you've permanently sworn off men. Tell me why."

I didn't miss the brief flicker of surprise in Jade's eyes. I certainly didn't miss the way she stiffened slightly in my arms. I barely heard it, but I didn't miss the hiss of her breath between her teeth.

She was quiet for a few beats, and then she shrugged. "What does it matter?"

I didn't know why it mattered to me, but it absolutely did.

Chapter Eleven

JADE

What does it matter?

My own question mocked me while we sat at a table during the reception. It didn't surprise me Walker had heard I didn't date. Stolen Hearts Valley was a small world. People talked. I also hadn't tried to keep it a secret. I'd stated my intentions and thrown it back into the faces of anyone who questioned me. Social expectations never sat well with me. People shouldn't be bound by what others expected of them. Women, especially, had spent so many centuries under the brutal thumb of social expectations largely dictated by men.

I wanted to be independent and sure as hell didn't appreciate people questioning that choice. I was fine. Better than fine. I savored my choice and the freedom of just not worrying about the whole stupid dating world.

And yet, here I was at a wedding where people were sighing and happily getting teary over the bride and groom. Dave and Jenny truly seemed to love each other, and it was lovely.

Based on the responses, I was pulling off a good little act with Walker of convincing people we were an actual couple, offering only the vaguest of details about meeting at Stolen Hearts Lodge and so on. The part that had me restlessly crossing and uncrossing my legs and shifting my shoulders was the fact it was definitely no act that I wanted him.

Hell, I *craved* him. Every little subtle touch was electrifying—his hand holding mine, his arm around my waist with his strong palm curled around my hip, and the feel of his lips pressing against my neck with a way too familiar kiss. Goose bumps rose on my skin, heat spun in pinwheels through my body, and desire fizzed in my veins with every chance look and touch.

Just now, I experienced a moment of feeling bereft when he leaned over to whisper in my ear in that sexy, gravelly voice of his that he needed to make a toast. He squeezed my shoulders before he stood, and I instantly missed his warm, strong presence.

He leaned down and said something to Dave before straightening and looking out over the crowd assembled in the room. Walker was rakishly handsome—with his dark hair, those smoke-silver eyes, and that quiet way of carrying himself. Before these last few days, I'd thought him reserved. I'd also been annoyed by him. I could barely, just barely, admit to myself that was because the attraction sizzled between us no matter what, and *that* annoyed me. It had tested my belief that I couldn't be affected like that.

Now, having spent more time with him, I'd seen a few more flashes of the man underneath the surface. Unfortunately for me, getting to know Walker only served to deepen my attraction to him. There *was* that kiss.

Just now, he cast a teasing smile toward Dave before he looked out over the crowd again. He didn't even have to clear his throat, or do anything else to silence the crowd. His presence alone demanded enough.

After the wedding ceremony, he'd done away with his tie, although he still had his suit jacket on. My eyes kept lingering on the deep bronze skin revealed against the crisp white shirt where he'd undone several buttons.

Casting his smile over the crowd, he lifted his champagne flute high. "Apparently, the best man is expected to give a toast. Although I never was that great at following convention." There were a few low chuckles that rumbled through the crowd at that. "Dave is my oldest and closest friend. If anyone deserves a toast after his wedding, it's him. To be quite honest, I was surprised when Dave first spoke to me about Jenny. As many of you know, Dave met Jenny while I was overseas. I didn't have a chance to do any vetting for him."

The crowd laughed again, and Walker glanced at Jenny. "Turns out, Dave didn't need me to vet Jenny. The first time I saw them together, I knew he was down for the count. If only, because Jenny is perfect for him. I'm not talking about how beautiful she is. That's obvious to anyone who sees her. I'm talking about the fact she can hold her own and brings out the best in him. Dave was a most excellent dedicated bachelor and is absolutely one of the most loyal and solid people I know. It stands to reason that if he's going to fall, he'll fall hard."

My chest tightened slightly. Although Walker's tone was light and teasing, I sensed he was dead serious underneath.

"I can't pretend to be an expert on love, although I suppose I could claim to be some sort of expert on Dave. I *have* known him since first grade. He was always a looker, even then." That comment got a good laugh from the crowd and an eye roll from Dave as Jenny leaned over to kiss his cheek. "I'll say this, I might have been surprised Dave fell in love, but I'm not surprised in the least that he fell for Jenny. And you, my dear, well, you found yourself the best kind of man. Those who matter to Dave matter forever. Welcome to the club, although you've been in it since the day he met you. I have absolutely no doubt you two will have a long and happy marriage. I also have no doubt there will be plenty of

arguments along the way. That's how Dave shows his love."
More laughter accompanied this along with a nod of agreement from Jenny. "I wish you nothing but happiness. Know
that to everyone who counts you as friends, we're rooting
for you. One last thing, Dave bet me that I believe in love.
When I asked why, he said it was because he knew I
believed in him and Jenny. And, I absolutely do. So if my
cynical heart can buy it, you can rest assured it's the real
deal."

At that, glasses were raised, mine included. Then, Walker
returned to my side, sliding his arm around my shoulders as
he set his champagne flute down on the table. I didn't quite
know how to read the expression in his eyes. I couldn't say I
knew him particularly well.

Yes, but you feel safe with him, a voice whispered deep in a
shadowed corner of my heart.

"How'd I do?" Walker asked.

It was just a question, a question that had nothing to do
with me. But still, a shiver chased over my skin at his drawl
and the rough edge to his voice that I was coming to love.

Restless, I uncrossed my legs and crossed the other one
over the top. "Quite well," I managed, my voice coming out
a little breathy.

"I think my duties are officially done, right? Or did I
miss a rule? There're so many unspoken rules to weddings
that I don't even know what the hell I'm really supposed
to do."

Walker's question was earnest, and I almost laughed.
Although Walker came across as a completely confident
man, it was becoming clear to me that when someone was
important to him, he wanted to make sure to do the right
thing even if he didn't know precisely what that was.

I nodded. "As far as I understand it—wedding etiquette,
that is—your duties are officially done. I don't even think
the toast was a given, but many best men do offer a toast.
Dave means a lot to you, doesn't he?"

I wasn't quite sure why that question slipped out, but it did.

Walker was quiet for a beat, and the teasing glint in his eyes faded. With a single, decisive nod, he replied, "Absolutely. He is truly my best friend. He's like a brother to me."

"Do you have any brothers and sisters?" I asked, forgetting for a second that I'd asked him that question on our drive here.

With the direction of the conversation, that was a logical question. Yet, the moment it passed across my lips, I suddenly knew that it was somehow loaded, and that Walker's cursory response during the drive wasn't the whole story. Of course, I didn't know why.

After a moment that felt jammed up by my question, Walker replied, "I didn't mention it when you asked before, but I had a little brother who died. It wasn't that I wanted to lie. It's just easier not to dive into it. You know?"

I managed, just barely, to contain my gasp and nodded jerkily. "I'm so sorry. I didn't know. I understand why you don't usually mention it to people." My mind spun in circles with the implication that he'd chosen to share this personal and sad detail with me.

His hand tightened incrementally where it was resting on my shoulder. "Of course you didn't know. How could you without me telling you? Thank you, though. He died when he was a baby. Apparently, he had a breathing disorder, but it wasn't diagnosed until he died in his sleep. It was a long time ago."

Unsure what else to say, I nodded and repeated, "I'm so sorry."

I felt the pads of his fingers press into the skin of my shoulder when he squeezed again. "It's okay. Really."

Someone else said something on Walker's opposite side, and he turned to reply. I reached for my champagne and took a gulp, savoring the fresh, bright burst of flavor. The waiter stopped by with a tray of glasses filled with champagne. I shook my head, and Walker leaned back, asking, "Can we have a fresh bottle, please?"

My chest tightened. Even though I'd commented to Walker last night about why I didn't prefer to have guys buy my drinks, it seemed his perception ran deeper. Somehow, he'd picked up that I didn't prefer to take a drink unless I knew exactly where it came from. The fact he made sure to take care of that had tears stinging at the backs of my eyes.

That led to me reminding myself, yet again, I was an emotional wreck over nothing.

Chapter Twelve

JADE

A few hours later, I walked at Walker's side up the stairs. This inn had only one elevator since it was an older building. When we noticed the line of people waiting for the elevator, we elected to take the stairs at the end of the hallway. It was only two flights.

Although I'd had a few glasses of champagne over the course of the evening, I wasn't drunk. If I'd ever been tipsy, that had worn off. As it was, my entire body felt as if it were fizzing like champagne—alive and bubbling from the sparks of need Walker elicited.

His hand was warm where it rested at the dip in my waist. I wished it would slide down over my bottom, and I was a bit startled at that. I wasn't prone to craving a man's touch, but Walker was proving to be the exception to many rules. We crested the landing between the second and third floors, and one of my heels caught on the carpet. When I stumbled slightly, he tightened his grip on my waist and steadied me.

"Easy there," he murmured.

Glancing up, I was instantly trapped in his gaze. My

mind whirled back to my reckless and impulsive kiss this morning. *Kiss him again.*

I was practically taunting myself. My pulse was racing along madly. It was quiet in the stairwell. After hours of voices and noise, it felt as if we'd stepped out of reality for just a moment.

Walker's gaze was darkening, like clouds burgeoning before a thunderstorm. He turned slightly, taking a step closer. I reflexively stepped back, not realizing the wall was right there behind me. My hips bumped against it. With my knees going wobbly at the look in Walker's eyes, I was relieved for the support. I couldn't look away and took a shallow breath as I swiped my tongue across my bottom lip.

"I need some clarification," he said, his tone gravelly and sending tingles spinning through me like hot flares.

"About what?" My question came out raspy. I mentally rolled my eyes at myself. All this time I'd been so confident no man could ever get to me.

My confidence was turning out to be so foolish. I'd been stupid enough to think I would never be tempted. I also knew ever since I'd first met Walker that he was like flint to stone for me, striking sparks all around me just for being close.

I vividly remembered the night I met him. I'd seen him in person here and there when I covered shifts at Lost Deer Bar before we officially met. He was usually hanging with my brother and the other guys from the first responder crew. I'd thought him handsome, but I'd bet anyone who could see probably thought that. One night, he'd given me a ride home after I got a flat tire in bad weather. I'd gotten up close and personal with the potency of his presence on that drive.

Even knowing the electric power of my body's reaction to him, I hadn't thought I would fall prey to a desire that practically glowed with heat. Yet, here I was. I knew my cheeks were flushed. The heat was intense, suffusing my entire being.

The only relief I could find from it was to dive straight into the heart of the fire. As these thoughts chased in circles in my mind, Walker's eyes searched my face.

After a long moment, he asked, "When you said we only have two nights, what did you mean?"

Oh God. He was going to make me say it out loud. I hated the sense of vulnerability this desire kindled inside of me. Pushing against it helped me get a hold of my gooey self. I felt like I was about to melt into a puddle at his feet. With his arm wrapped around my waist, and his strong body pressed close to my side, all of it was overwhelming.

Narrowing my eyes, I scrambled for some control and told myself I wasn't going to be a coward. "Just that. I won't pretend I don't want you, although it annoys the hell out of me. But we're here, and we're sharing a room, so let's take advantage of the circumstances. Let's not make it anything more than that."

Walker was quiet for several thumps of my heart before a slow smile stretched from one corner of his mouth to the other. Oh hell. His smiles were dangerous. My belly felt all fluttery and my breath got shallow.

He looked as if he was considering something. I suddenly recalled his comment about my brother. Straightening my shoulders against the wall behind me, I lifted my chin. "Don't you dare include my brother's potential opinion in this equation. We're two consenting adults, and this is none of his fucking business."

Walker's responding slow laugh sent a hot shiver through me. I shifted my weight on my feet. I knew things were bad when I could feel the slick heat between my thighs. We hadn't even kissed yet, and I was already so turned on, there was a throb at my core.

"Obviously, I'm aware it's not really any of his business. Just as I'm aware if your brother finds out, I'll probably get his fist in my face."

That infuriated me. There was only one person who had a say in what I did with my body. That person was me.

Driven by the tumultuous combination of the simmering desire that needed a relief valve and irritation at the knowledge my brother most likely would have an opinion if he knew anything about this, I hooked my index finger over the last closed button on Walker's shirt. His skin was warm against my knuckle. There was no tie for me to yank off, since he'd divested himself of that hours ago, so this would have to do.

When I pulled him closer, Walker rested a hand on the wall, just beside my shoulder as the full heat and strength of his body covered mine from head to toe.

"I didn't say that would stop me," he murmured right before our lips collided.

As wild as I felt inside, our kiss burst into flames, rushing like a brush fire. Walker angled his head to the side as I arched into him, gasping when he fit his mouth over mine and swept his tongue inside. After a deep sweep of his tongue against mine, he drew back, gentling our kiss just as quickly. He dusted a kiss on one corner of my mouth and then the other, turning my insides to molten lava.

Electricity was zinging through my body so fast, I couldn't contain it. My legs shifted and my hips rocked into the hard, hot press of Walker's arousal, which was cradled at my hips. I whimpered when he brushed his lips across mine and teased my tongue with his again.

In another hot second, our kiss was all-consuming. Walker was a master at kissing, his hand sliding into my hair as he angled my head just so to most effectively plunder my mouth with sensual, maddening strokes of his tongue. By the time he pulled back again, lightly catching my bottom lip with his teeth, it was a good thing I had the wall behind me. Without it, I almost certainly would have collapsed.

While we stood there, I could feel the rapid beat of his heart where his chest was pressed against mine. My own heartbeat was totally out of control, and I had to gulp air with messy breaths. The sound of footsteps coming up the first flight of stairs below us barely filtered through the haze in my mind.

Walker gave his head a shake and straightened. "Let's go."

I'd never had this kind of experience where I didn't want any physical distance between us. Whether Walker felt the same or not, he kept his arm around me as he guided me up the next flight of stairs. His hand slid lower on my waist, and his fingers splayed over the curve of my bottom. I savored every point of contact. His touch was like a brand on me. The brush of his hips against mine was warm with each step, and the curve of his shoulder sheltered me as we moved in unison.

I couldn't tell you if we moved quickly or not. I was in a haze, an almost dream-like state, with every cell in my body vibrating with anticipation.

Just before we reached our room, someone said Walker's name. I reflexively followed his gaze as he paused and angled back to look over his shoulder. Dave and Jenny stood there at the end of the hallway.

"Just wanted to say thanks, man," Dave called. "Don't forget what I said earlier."

A grin stretched across Walker's face. "Of course not. We'll see you in the morning, right?"

"You sure will," Jenny replied with a smile. At that, they waved and turned to step into what I presumed was the honeymoon suite.

The heat banked in Walker's eyes nearly took my breath away. "Shall we?"

I couldn't even speak and simply nodded. Walker propelled me forward with a gentle, coaxing pressure. There were only a few more feet to our door. Seeing as I didn't even know where my key card was, I was relieved Walker quickly produced his from the pocket inside his suit jacket. Seconds later, the door was clicking shut behind us.

In a flash, Walker had turned and pressed me against the door. "Now, where were we?" he murmured, right before his mouth claimed mine again in a kiss for the ages.

By the time we came up for air, I was positive that particular kiss needed to be documented in some history book. If there was a history book of kisses, a chapter should be dedicated to Walker's kisses. Hot, wet, teasing, and sensual, his kisses overpowered all of my senses and left me in a puddle of want.

Although it had been a while since I'd been intimate with anyone, I knew exactly what I wanted. Walker. Naked. Now.

Chapter Thirteen

WALKER

When Jade moaned into our kiss, what little control I had almost snapped. She arched her hips against me, and I became painfully aware of just how deeply I wanted her. I was rock-hard, my cock swollen and tight in my dress slacks. Ever since I'd zipped up her dress hours and hours ago, I'd been in a state of unsettled arousal.

Her mouth was warm and pliant under mine, and her tongue was a maddening tease. My fingers curled against the door as one of her hands deftly unbuttoned my shirt. When her warm palm coasted over my skin as she pushed it out of the way, it was a special form of hell.

Maybe I was crazy enough to ignore the fact Lucas would have my head if he knew I had my hands all over his sister, but I definitely didn't think he would appreciate that Jade already drew clear lines around what we could have. To make matters worse, the burning need I felt for Jade was unrivaled. I couldn't stop it, or contain it.

She wore this soft silky dress that flowed over her curves. Now that she was plastered against me, I was acutely aware of just how good she felt. I could feel the press of her tight nipples against me, and the moist heat at the apex of her thighs. Her tongue teased sensually with mine, and the sounds she made in the back of her throat had my balls tightening.

I could feel myself almost stumbling internally with lust whipping through me like a storm. Needing something, anything, to help me regain control, I tore my lips free from hers and pressed hot kisses along her jawline. I slid my hand down her side, savoring the soft give of her flesh. I gave into the urge and coasted my palm over her belly before sliding up.

Jade was a mixture of tomboy and deep femininity. I could feel the strength of her body in every move she made, and yet, her curves were generous. The weight of her breast in my palm was delicious. The sound of her breath catching in her throat when I teased my thumb over the taut peak of her nipple nearly undid me.

She murmured something indecipherable, and I lifted my head. "Yes?" I lightly squeezed my thumb and forefinger around her nipple.

Jade's dark hair was falling around her shoulders in a messy tousle. Her lips were swollen and pink, and I wanted to pull her dress up around her waist and fuck her right here and right now against the door. Her head fell back with a soft thump. Her breasts rose and fell with every ragged breath.

When she didn't respond, I prompted, "You said something?"

"You have too many clothes on," she announced.

Her tone was bossy, but also husky and so damn sexy, the sound of it alone was a light lash of the whip driving my desire.

I chuckled, squeezing her nipple once more before releasing it reluctantly. "Well, that's something we can agree on."

Jade's throaty laugh nearly snatched back what little control I'd gained in the last few moments.

"I'm sure we can agree on a lot more than that." She put her palm on my bare chest and pushed me away from her. I had two warring impulses. I didn't want to move away from her delectable body, and yet I wanted *more*, so *much* more.

Although my body was restless and impatient for everything, for all of Jade, I wanted to savor this. Of late, sex had been mostly a practical matter for me. My mind flashed to Dave's reminder about what he said about love to me. Although I believed Dave loved Jenny, I wasn't quite sure I believed in the possibility of love for myself. I kept things practical. I was all about casual friends with benefits. It worked for me.

I shied away from contemplating where Jade fit in. The ferocity of how much I wanted her was downright shocking. And yet, I wanted to enjoy it, to take it for what it was.

A distant corner of my mind called out a warning shout. There was something else here, something shimmering under the surface of the potent and fiery desire between us.

I ignored it for now. Because Jade was moving, calling over her shoulder, "Come 'ere."

I didn't usually prefer to take orders, but when they were coming from Jade in her breathy, sexy voice, I would do anything she asked. Anything at all. She might as well have had a leash attached to me. I turned and followed her across the room. She stopped at the foot of the bed to kick off her low-heeled sandals.

"Need a little help?" I asked from behind her, lifting her hair and pushing it over her shoulder.

"Please." She bowed her head, and I caught the tab of the zipper. The soft sound it made as I drew it down spun into the vibration humming in the air around us.

The fabric fell open, and I released her hair to slide my hands up and curl them over her shoulders. She started to turn around.

"Not yet." My words were a soft command, and she obeyed, holding still as I dipped my head and dropped hot, openmouthed kisses along the back of her neck.

Her skin rose in goose bumps under my lips. I slid a hand down her spine, satisfaction rolling through me when she trembled slightly under my touch.

Jade was a controlled, guarded woman, and most definitely on the prickly, standoffish side. She didn't give off any vibe of innocence. It was more than clear to me that the honor of touching her was something I had to earn.

Her dress fell in a rumple around her waist, and I stroked my hands around her waist from behind, my arousal pressed between the cheeks of her bottom through the fabric. Her breath came in rapid, shallow pants. All the while, need clawed at me. It was almost painful to keep myself in check. That was how fiercely I wanted her.

Her skin was silky soft. I groaned at the feel of her nipples pebbling under my touch and let my teeth graze lightly on her neck, just a little nip. She trembled again and cried my name on the heels of a ragged gasp.

"Sugar, you're fucking killin' me."

Jade suddenly turned in my arms, her eyes wide and dark. "I need you," she murmured as her hand slid around my nape. She yanked me down for a messy kiss, and we fell on the bed in a tangle. Jade kicked her dress free, greeting me with the sight of a pair of bright purple cotton panties, so incongruous in contrast to the silky confection of her dress. I almost laughed.

Pushing away, I stood quickly and toed my shoes off while she shoved my shirt off my shoulders. I didn't bother with my slacks yet. I sensed if I stripped down right away, this would be over in a matter of minutes.

Jade caught my eyes as she leaned back on her elbows on the mattress. "Do you like my panties?" she teased.

I arched a brow and cocked my head to the side, letting my eyes lazily trail up from her bright purple toenails to her matching cotton panties before making my way to her face. "Very practical."

"You didn't answer my question."

"So I didn't. Yes, I love them."

I stretched out beside her, leaning around to catch her nipple in my mouth and giving it a quick suck. Lifting my head, I said, "Now, be quiet. I'm not in the mood to chat."

"I can't talk at all?" she murmured, gasping when I swirled my tongue around her other nipple.

"You can talk all you want, just no quizzes."

Jade, typically so guarded and prickly, released a low chuckle. Something about her letting go, even if not completely, spurred on the intense drive to claim her, to make her mine. That desire should've given me pause. I'd never wanted to claim any woman in my life, much less considered any woman in a possessive manner. And yet, Jade had that effect on me. She was a challenge, and I'd never backed down from a challenge. Teasing her nipples, I barely kept my own need in check as she writhed under my attentions.

Lifting my head after a last swirl of my tongue around one of her tight, dark pink nipples, I was gratified to see her dragging her eyes open to half mast and her breath coming in ragged gasps. With her skin flushed pink, her lips slightly parted, and her dark tresses spread out against the pillows, she was a sight to behold.

"So fucking sexy," I whispered as I leaned up and lightly nipped at the soft skin just behind her ear.

Goose bumps broke out over her skin and her hips arched against me where I was half lying over her. I kept moving, blazing a damp trail down the valley between her breasts while I teased one nipple with my thumb. I dropped hot kisses over her belly, and she trembled under my touch. She was restless, her strong, lush body shifting as I made my way down.

I trailed my fingers over the damp folds between her thighs, prompting her to cry out. "Walker!"

"Mmmhmm?" My lips moved against her skin with my murmured query.

I hooked a finger over the edge of that purple cotton. Pushing it to the side, I almost groaned out loud at the feel of her slick, wet heat.

Whatever she meant to say was lost in a sharp gasp followed by a moan. While there were many things I wanted to savor, wasting time getting Jade completely naked wasn't something I cared to bother with. I yanked her panties roughly down her legs. She helpfully kicked them free of her ankles as I shifted farther down on the mattress.

I was greeted with another breathy gasp when I teased her folds, the juice of her arousal coating my fingers.

"Walker, please..."

Her words were lost in another moan as I finally, *finally*, gave in to the urge to taste her. Her scent and flavor assailed me, salty sweet, somehow exactly like her personality. As I explored her folds with my tongue, barely glancing over the hot button of need at her core, I sank one finger and then another inside of her.

Her channel rippled around me as I set myself to the task to drive her wild. She flexed under my touch with each rock of her hips. Little sounds came from her throat, swelling my cock to the point I thought I might explode from the pressure.

On the heels of a deep drive of my fingers stretching into her channel, I dragged my tongue over her clit, and she cried out sharply. Her entire body rippled and her channel clenched around my fingers.

Lifting my head, I soaked in the sight of Jade completely undone. Her head had fallen back against the pillows, and her body was covered in a sheen of light sweat. I slowly drew my fingers out of her core as her trembling eased.

Reversing course, I mapped my way back up her body,

unable to resist dusting kisses over her belly. I caught a nipple lightly in my mouth before pressing kisses along the side of her neck, savoring the goose bumps rising under my touch. I settled onto an elbow, my arousal insistent and impatient as my cock throbbed.

Jade's green eyes opened slowly, an almost dazed look in them. I had to admit, I felt a surge of masculine pride that I could bring her to this point.

Her lips curled at the corners in a lazy smile. "Well, Walker, you've set a high bar."

I opened my mouth to reply when there was a sharp knock at our hotel room door. Jade rolled her head to the side, actually glaring at the door. Turning back, her voice was husky when she spoke. "Who the hell could that be?"

I cupped her breast in my palm, savoring its lush weight and the way it filled my hand perfectly. "Hell if I know. I think we should ignore it. I'm certainly not expecting anyone. Are you?"

Her throaty chuckle tightened my need for her. "Uh, I'm your wedding guest. You're more likely to have someone banging on our door."

I dipped my head to press a kiss on the side of her neck, masking my chuckle. Although I was awash in the scent and feel of Jade, a part of me was rattled and unsettled by this easy comfort between us.

There was another knock at the door, followed by a male voice calling my name. Lifting my head, I met Jade's eyes and sighed. "I think I should answer."

"Go on, get the door," she urged.

Shifting to my side, I ran a hand through my hair. "I'm not exactly in a state to answer the door."

Jade nudged her hip slightly against my blatant erection. "Put your pants on. By the time you get to the door, no one will be able to notice. I'll go in the bathroom."

I thought she meant to be helpful, but the sight of Jade's lithe and lush body climbing out of bed and walking into the bathroom did nothing to help tamp down my ardor. She leaned around the corner of the bathroom door, her dark hair falling over one shoulder. "Hurry up," she mouthed as someone knocked on the door yet again.

"Coming!" I called out.

I did as Jade instructed and yanked on my dress slacks and even tossed on my shirt for good measure. As I'd predicted, it didn't help all that much with my arousal. Although by the time I swung the door open, I didn't think anyone would notice with the ends of my shirt hanging down.

"What's going on?" I asked before I even had the door fully open and saw the guy standing on the other side. It was Dave's brother, Steve, with a pained expression on his face. "Hey, what is it?" I instantly sobered.

His face was white, drawn into tense lines. He shook his head. "Dave collapsed."

My brain didn't compute the ramifications. "I'm sorry, what?"

"Dave collapsed. He's on the way to the hospital."

"When and where?"

"Jenny called from the room. He's alive in the ambulance, and Jenny's with him. When I couldn't find you in the reception, I figured you must've already come up to your room. I'm sorry to interrupt, but I figured you would want to know."

"Where is the hospital?" My words were clipped, but I didn't care to make polite conversation.

"About five miles away. I'm headed down there with my parents now. Not that I think you're concerned, but Dee won't be there. I know she's been a pain, so I asked her to stay out of it."

That was the last thing on my mind, and if Dee had been there, I would've ignored her. But I didn't even care about that right now. I simply nodded. "Text me the address. I'll meet y'all there."

Chapter Fourteen

JADE

I held the paper coffee cup under the dispenser, feeling my hand warming as coffee filled the cup. Setting one down, I filled the next. After that, I added a dash of cream to mine and stuffed some sugar packets and creamers in my pockets. Although Walker now held the honor of being the only man to bring me to climax, I didn't know how he liked his coffee.

It was past midnight, and the hospital was largely quiet, yet it felt as if the entire place was humming. No matter where I walked, I could hear distant machines and the low murmur of voices from the nursing stations on every floor.

I was relieved I'd thought to pack something casual that I figured I would only be wearing on the drive home. My tennis shoes barely made a sound as I walked briskly down the hallway. My faded, worn jeans were comfortable, especially with the chill in the air-conditioned building.

I slowed as I approached the waiting area. When I rounded the corner and saw Walker sitting against the far wall with his elbows braced on his knees and his head hanging down, my heart squeezed. Ever since the interruption earlier tonight, Walker had been a bundle of tension and worry.

If I hadn't guessed it before, I knew he was a man accustomed to carrying things alone. It was so clear he loved Dave in the way not many men love their friends. We still didn't have any news on Dave's condition, and Walker had been quiet and drawn since we arrived at the hospital.

He'd seemed startled when I had popped out of the bathroom and quickly tugged on my clothes. I wasn't going to let him go to the hospital by himself. Crossing the room, I slipped into the chair beside him. Dave's brother had left a few minutes ago to go back to the hotel and provide the lack of an update to the guests waiting for any morsel of news ever since Dave collapsed in his hotel room after the reception.

Dave's parents were sitting at an angle across from Walker and me. Their hands were clasped together. His mother had finally fallen into a restless sleep with her head against her husband's shoulder after the hospital had given her something to relax since she was so distraught. Jenny was dozing in another chair with her mother flipping through magazines at her side.

"Here," I said softly.

Walker lifted his head, his eyes catching mine. "Thanks," he said gruffly as he took the coffee from me.

I fished the sugar and creamers out of my pocket and held them out on my flat palm. "I didn't know if you wanted sugar or cream."

The barest hint of a smile flashed across his face as he shook his head. "Neither, but thank you."

Without thinking, I rested my palm on the center of his back, rubbing it in a slow circle.

Walker looked over again. "Thanks for being here."

"Of course."

I had to admit this was all rather strange. Walker and I'd been deeply intimate hours earlier. And yet, somehow these last few hours that had passed together, I felt closer to him than I'd felt to anyone outside of my family. Ever. It was a different kind of closeness. Witnessing someone in a state of worry and concern and having them allow you to be there in quiet support was intense.

Walker took a long swallow of the mediocre coffee. "If you'd rather head back to the hotel and get some sleep, I understand."

I took a sip of my coffee before shaking my head. "I wouldn't sleep anyway. I'd rather be here."

He held my gaze for a few beats before dipping his head in a nod. "Thank you," was all he said in return.

With the television in the corner of the waiting room rumbling on whatever news they had to discuss at this hour, Walker and I waited together. I didn't know how much more time passed before the doctor came into the waiting area.

It felt as if we'd been collectively wrapped in a cocoon of worry and concern. The appearance of the doctor jolted all of us into an edgy wakefulness. Walker stood quickly, along with Dave's father. He turned back to give a gentle squeeze to Dave's mother's shoulder, leaning down to whisper in her ear. She stood just as Jenny jerked awake and staggered up from her chair. Jenny's mother steadied her and crossed the room with her.

We'd seen this doctor earlier when he stopped in to let us know Dave was stable, and they were going to assess what was going on. All we knew was Dave had a heart attack, and they were going to operate.

Walker reached for my hand when he stood. It was only as we were walking across the waiting area together that I realized we'd definitely appear to be a couple to anyone who saw us. I hadn't even thought twice about letting him curl his strong hand around mine. I gave a squeeze in return, a small effort to impart some strength to him.

"How is he?" Walker asked immediately, just as Dave's parents reached the doctor.

The doctor looked amongst everyone and nodded firmly. "He's going to be fine. I'm sorry I couldn't give you more information earlier. Honestly, given Dave's age, I wasn't prepared to say more until we operated."

"Well?" Dave's mother's voice was hoarse from the tears she'd cried earlier.

Jenny stayed quiet, but her eyes were wide.

"As I said, he had a heart attack. Dave is a lucky man. He survived what's known as a widow maker. That's a blockage in his left anterior artery, the one going down. Those tend to result in heart attacks that are abrupt and seem to come out of nowhere. He had an almost complete blockage. A blockage that complete at his age is concerning. We fully repaired it and cleared the artery. He will need to be mindful of his diet for the rest of his life. He'll make a full recovery and live a healthy life. Although it's not too common for someone his age to have a heart attack like that, his age will help him stay healthy and shorten his recovery time." The doctor looked toward Jenny. "Your new husband will be back on his feet soon."

Jenny burst into tears, and her mother pulled her into a hug. While Jenny sniffled and dabbed at her eyes with a tissue, the doctor continued to rattle off information.

By the time we were walking out of the hospital, Walker was practically sagging at my side. When we got to his truck, I held my hand out, gesturing with my fingers. "Give me the keys. I'm driving. You're too tired." When he lifted his head and opened his mouth to argue, I simply shook my head. "Seriously, Walker."

"You've got to be just as tired as me," he muttered.

"Although we've both been awake for the same amount of time, this has been an emotional blow for you. I just met Dave this weekend, and he's been your best friend for years. That counts. Don't go thinking you can fight me on this. I'll kick your butt with how tired you are."

For the first time in hours, a smile split across Walker's

face. "If I recall," he drawled, "the last time you found yourself in the middle of a fight, I had to help you out."

I threw my head back with a laugh, just before reaching to snatch the keys out of his hand. I nudged him on the shoulder and even opened the passenger door for him. He rolled his eyes, but he climbed in.

Once I was in the driver's seat, I adjusted the seat and took a gander at the dashboard and various controls before tapping the start button.

"Are you one of those guys who worries about someone else driving your truck?" I asked conversationally as I put it in gear and slowly backed out of the parking space.

He chuckled. It said something about the depth of my attraction to him that despite how out of place it was and despite how weary we both were, the mere sound of his gruff laugh sent a prickle down my spine and heat racing over the surface of my skin.

"No. I'm not one of those guys. If it was a stick shift and you couldn't drive that, well, then I might be worried."

"It's not a stick shift, but I could handle it if it was. My father insisted Lucas and I learn. It was only a few years ago that Lucas finally got over his snobbery about that and got a regular automatic truck."

Walker laughed again. "I get it. I was the same way. Damn stupid. Shifting gears takes work."

After I turned onto the road that would take us back to the wedding hotel, I commented, "I'm glad Dave's going to be okay."

I felt Walker's sigh to my depths. It was so heartfelt when his head fell back against the seat. "Yeah. He's like a brother to me. Thanks again for waiting with me tonight."

"Anytime."

We fell into silence for the remainder of the drive back to the hotel.

Walker was asleep when I parked the truck. Moonlight fell through the window, illuminating his profile. He was a beautiful man with strong, sculpted features. The tension he usually held in his features was gone in sleep. I wanted to lean over and kiss his cheek.

I didn't. I was unsettled tonight, completely thrown off my axis. Between experiencing my first climax with a man, and then being present on the heels of a frightening emergency, it was a lot to take in. I'd glimpsed the vulnerability that lay behind Walker's quiet exterior. It felt as if someone had taken tiny pry bars to the walls I'd built around my heart.

That unsettled feeling drove me to leap out of the truck, catching myself in time before I slammed the door behind me. Rounding to the passenger side, I opened the door quietly. "Walker." I shook him gently on the shoulder.

He mumbled something in his sleep before falling right back into it. I shook him again, this time saying his name at a higher volume. I'd carry him if I could, but I knew that was impossible.

"Huh?" he mumbled as his eyes finally opened. He rolled his head to the side, opening his eyes slowly. "Did I fall asleep?"

I smiled. "Yep. Come on, let's get you to bed."

A few minutes later, we were back in the hotel room. Walker kicked his shoes off, stumbling slightly. I caught him at the elbow to steady him. "You need to get in bed."

"That's what I was aiming for," he muttered with a sleepy smile.

Without further ado, he yanked his T-shirt off and shoved his jeans down, basically falling onto the bed as he kicked them free of his feet. Meanwhile, my mouth went dry at the sight of a shirtless Walker. Dear God. The man needed to come with a list of warnings—might blind you with hotness, don't touch or you'll get burned, melting imminent. Something along those lines.

Closing my eyes, I took a deep breath as I turned away. I made sure the door was locked, and set my purse down on the dresser. Walker was already sound asleep. He'd managed to crawl up to the pillows, but he hadn't even gotten under the covers. The sheets and comforter were still rumpled from our earlier encounter. He was half on his stomach with one knee bent up and his elbow tucked under the pillow. Jesus, even his ass was all muscle. His back was cut and every muscle was delineated even when he was relaxed.

As my eyes trailed down his body, they snagged on a thin scar that wrapped around from his back along his rib cage. I couldn't help but wonder what happened. I was starting to want to know far too much about Walker.

When I had agreed to this silly, fake wedding date, I chalked up my attraction to him as just a passing thing. Like lightning that struck once on a hot summer day with no storm to follow in its wake.

The more time I spent with him, the more I liked him. Stepping to the side of the bed, I carefully tucked the covers over him, unable to resist the urge to brush the dark lock that had fallen over his forehead out of his eyes.

With my heart tumbling in an unsteady beat, I went into the bathroom, taking a cool shower to wash away the sterile, antiseptic stickiness clinging to me from the hospital.

———

I came awake to the feel of Walker's muscled body curled around me from behind. His hard arousal pressed against my bottom, and I could feel the slick heat between my thighs. I decided I wanted to return a favor. Well, that was how I tried to rationalize it. I just wanted to touch Walker, and I wasn't quite ready to let myself think it ran deeper.

My thoughts glanced off the curious detail that last night I'd been fully prepared to take things all the way. Somehow, my awareness of my vulnerability intimidated me. When I felt intimidated, I had one response—to take control.

Moving carefully, I rolled over. Walker was deeply asleep. Yet, when I rose up on an elbow, I found his eyes opening. For a moment, they were hazed with sleep but then they widened. "Jade," was all he said.

Of course, he had to go say it in his gruff, gravelly, oh-so-sexy voice. I smiled, leaning over to string kisses over his chest and abdomen as I slid my palm down to cup the hard, hot length of his cock.

His breath came out in a hiss when I hooked my fingers over his fitted boxer briefs and pulled them down. His cock sprang free, long and thick, a little drop of pre-cum glistening on the tip.

"Jade, you don't..." His words ended in a groan when I leaned down to lick that salty drop and swirl my tongue around his cock head.

I didn't know what he'd tried to say, but he was a quick study. When I dragged my tongue along the underside of his shaft, his fingers laced in my hair on the heels of a ragged breath.

Shifting to my knees, I leaned down to take him fully in my mouth. My tongue slid back and forth as I drew upward again, curling my fist lightly around his cock. I felt a surge of power when his hips flexed up with each stroke of my grip, his cock bumping against the back of my throat.

When I moved upward, giving a little suction, my name came in a rough shout as his release spurted into my mouth. I waited until he had stopped shuddering, and then rose up slowly on my knees, looking down at him.

The sheets were fisted in his free hand, and he slowly released the other one from my hair. He stroked through my locks with his fingers brushing against my back and sending goose bumps skating over the surface of my skin.

"Come 'ere," he murmured with a light tug on my hair.

This all felt like *too* much, like *so* much more than I'd bargained for. I tried to play it light and smiled and shook my head.

"Jade, it's never a one-way street for me," he murmured before he reached between my thighs. With no preliminary, he pushed my panties to the side and stroked his fingers through my soaking wet folds.

I bit my lip, but I couldn't hold back. I cried out when he sank one long, thick finger inside, another immediately joining it.

Walker's touch was crazy fuel to my fire. I was drenched and already on the edge just from giving him pleasure. I wanted to look away from the intensity in his eyes, but I was locked in. It felt as if an electric current was running between us. With me on my knees above him, he fucked me with his fingers. He was gentle and rough at once. He finally released my hair to lightly cup one of my breasts through my T-shirt, teasing my nipple as he drove me to madness.

"Come on, Jade," he whispered. "Come for me."

As if I'd do anything but that. I couldn't have denied him

if I wanted to. Caught in his sensual gaze with every stroke of his fingers inside of me, his thumb teased over my clit. Pleasure scattered through me as everything tightened in my core. My eyes finally fell closed and pleasure burst like fireworks inside.

I distantly heard him saying, "That's it, sugar."

I shuddered so hard from the aftershocks of pleasure that I collapsed against him. He held me close. I tucked my head into his neck as I tried to catch my breath.

When I lifted my head and found his silver-smoke gaze waiting, my heart split wide-open. It wasn't just tiny pry bars to the walls around my heart anymore. With his touch, with his eyes, with who he was, Walker demolished them.

Chapter Sixteen

WALKER

"How the hell are you feeling?" I asked.

Dave sounded a little tired, but otherwise okay, when he laughed. The sound carried through the phone line with a hitch of static in the middle. "I've been better, but I've also been worse."

Emotion tightened in my throat. I didn't like contemplating the reality that Dave could have easily died that night. It had been a full two weeks since the wedding, and I'd yet to shake the unsettled feeling his heart attack had left behind for me.

"You have certainly been worse, and I'm so damn glad you survived. Seriously, though, you doing okay?" I pressed.

"Oh yeah. I really am. Don't get me wrong, that scared the shit out of me. I sure as hell never expected to have a heart attack on my wedding night, and that's not even considering that I'm only thirty-three years old."

I took a breath, letting it out slowly as I leaned against the wall in a half finished cabin where I was helping Wade, Jackson, and Lucas with construction for the lodge. Dave's call had come through right before I started to walk out with the guys to grab an early dinner in the staff kitchen. I'd waved them on, wanting a few minutes of privacy to talk with Dave.

"I'm just glad you're alive, which sounds morbid, but I mean it. How's Jenny taking everything?"

Although I couldn't see him, I could practically feel Dave's gaze sober through the phone line. "She's fine. I mean, she was pretty shaken up, along with, I guess, everybody. Instead of our honeymoon, she's been fussing over me at home. She's also thrilled to have a reason to force me to eat healthy," he said, finishing with a small laugh.

"Oh, I'll just bet. Although, you were never good about eating healthy. I get to say it now because you just had a freaking heart attack."

"I know. That's what I keep telling her. The doctor made it crystal clear that at my age, it's clear I had a predisposition for heart disease. Eating healthy will help me keep it under control, but it's something I'm gonna have to manage no matter what for the rest of my life," he explained with a sigh.

Rolling on my shoulder, I glanced out the framed window space that didn't yet have an actual glass window installed. This row of new cabins offered a spectacular view of Stolen Hearts Valley. With it being late spring, wildflowers were in bloom in the field just in front the lodge with the green of the trees expanding beyond that. The setting sun glinted off a lake over to the side and left a watercolor of pinks and purples above the mountain ridge on the opposite side of the valley.

"How's Jade?" Dave asked, deftly shifting the conversation.

"As far as I know, she's fine. I haven't seen her since the wedding. You know she was just there as a favor for me."

I could hear the sarcasm in Dave's laugh. "Right. You keep telling yourself that. I saw the way you looked at her. And Jenny saw the way she looked at you. Jenny also told me that Jade stayed with you in the waiting area for hours at the hospital."

Dave couldn't see me, but I rolled my eyes, hard enough to express my point even if it was only to myself. "Whatever, man."

Denial was a handy coping skill, and it was working for me.

"Well, when you do see her, give her my regards." I heard him shift the phone away and say something to someone in the background. His voice returned. "Jenny says hello. I gotta go. We're having dinner with her parents."

"Got it. I'll catch you later. Take care of yourself. For real."

"On it. Talk soon."

After we ended the call, I pushed away from the wall, leaning both hands in the open windowsill as I surveyed the view. Although I had considered a number of options when I left the military, I'd craved the familiar and soothing comfort of the Blue Ridge Mountains. Stolen Hearts Valley offered that sense of being home once again.

I'd needed that. As an Air Force pilot during two tours of duty overseas, I'd seen my share of the world. I'd also seen my share of things I preferred to forget. I had a good handle on them, or so I told myself. Something about Dave's heart attack had torn at those memories with sharp claws.

Dave was my oldest friend, and a few of the guys I served with were also like brothers to me. One of them, Keith, was gone. No matter how many times I told myself intellectually that I couldn't have changed that outcome, I wished I could have.

I didn't like being reminded of mortality and just how brutally people could be ripped away from you. Keith had a wife and a young son. I would've traded places with him. Ever since then, I'd promised myself I wouldn't let myself get too close to anyone. Although I was no longer working and living in a war zone, being a first responder and dealing with dicey rescue situations was part of my life. I couldn't imagine changing that. I derived a sense of purpose and focus from that work. Although I doubted I could ever save enough people to make up for the one friend I hadn't been able to save, I would keep trying.

As I turned away from the view with my boots echoing on the floor of the unfinished cabin, Jade swung the door open into my mind. She boldly walked through with her confident, take-no-shit stride. In my mind, she was usually wearing fitted jeans and those worn cowboy boots she favored. She'd been wearing those boots the very first time I met her when I gave her a ride home on that icy cold winter night.

A new vision of her had begun to replace that one. Just now, another one filled my mind—the sight of her on her knees above me with her nipples pressing against the thin cotton of her T-shirt as she threw her head back and came all over my fingers. The mere recollection of that moment sent a shot of blood to my groin. Fuck me.

I didn't enjoy thinking about it, but it wasn't just Dave's heart attack that had left me unsettled lately. Much as I wanted to deny it, the sly voice inside my head occasionally felt the need to remind me that perhaps it was my reaction to Jade that had knocked me off balance and left me scrambling for purchase. Take now, for example.

You know you want her. Why don't you do something about it?

It was bad enough already. If her brother found out that I was going after Jade for nothing more than scratching that itch and seeing things through all the way, he'd fucking kill me. Okay, so maybe Lucas wouldn't kill me, but he definitely might throw a solid punch right to my jaw.

You know it's not just sex you're after. What are you so afraid of?

My mind was taunting me. I was walking alone through the trees, and I shook my head at myself, murmuring, "Shut the fuck up." That's what Jade reduced me to—talking to myself.

I stepped through the trees with the main lodge coming into view. There were two old barns that had been renovated entirely. One of them had a restaurant in the downstairs with the hotel upstairs, while the other was all guest lodging with high-end fancy rooms, skylights, and glorious views of the Blue Ridge Mountains everywhere you looked.

I angled toward the back end of one of the barns. The lodge restaurant was busy and not just for guests. North Carolina was a foodie state, and the mountains were home to plenty of restaurants that graced the pages of dining websites and magazines. Jackson had been smart to plan a restaurant as part of the resort. He couldn't have counted on how well it would do under the steady hand of Dani's management.

Working at the lodge had a major, and I do mean *major*, perk. Although I didn't live here, I still got to join in on staff meals whenever I wanted. While guests dined on amazing fare, Dani made sure the staff also had food for lunch and dinner. Lunch was more casual, but dinner was usually a step up.

I pushed through the back door into the staff kitchen, relieved at the sound of voices reaching my ears. Not because I was the most social or chatty kind of guy, but rather because the distraction of company would perhaps kick Jade out of my thoughts.

Just as I walked from the back hallway into the staff area, a dish towel landed on my shoulder, coming from the center of the room where there was a large table. Lifting the towel off my shoulder, I held it up. "Anyone need this?"

Evie grinned as she waved in my direction. "Nope. Just my bad aim. If you don't mind leaving it in the laundry right there, I'd sure appreciate it, Walker."

"You got it," I replied as I tossed it into the laundry bin by the door.

Jackson glanced over from across the room where he

stood by the counter pouring himself a cup of coffee. "Coffee?" he called.

"Sure thing."

Crossing the room to him, I felt a prickle at the back of my neck. Without even looking, I knew Jade was here. She wasn't here that often. In fact, the last time I recalled her being here was when her car broke down on that winter night. The very first time I met her.

She'd seared herself into my memory that night, but now it was worse, much, much worse. I knew what she looked like flying apart. I knew the feel of her lips moving under mine and the sounds she made when she tumbled over the edge into her release. I also knew exactly how her lips felt wrapped around my cock as she teased me to madness with her tongue.

I couldn't have stopped myself from looking over my shoulder if I tried. I didn't even bother to try. Because I wanted to see her. I *craved* seeing her.

My eyes found her immediately. She stood beside the picnic style table at the back of the kitchen. She wore jeans and those cowboy boots with a loose white blouse.

She was talking to Lucas. Her brother's presence did nothing to tamp my body's response at simply seeing her. A jolt of electricity spun through me. As if sensing my eyes on her, our gazes collided. It felt as if a thin flame rose in the air between us, a streak of fire licking its way across the room.

"Walker." Jackson's voice nudged me out of that temporary heated moment.

I tore my eyes away from Jade with a sharp nod in greeting before looking back at Jackson.

"Got your coffee," he said as I began moving again. I hadn't even noticed I'd come to a complete stop when I caught sight of Jade. That was not good, not good at all.

When I reached Jackson, I took the mug of coffee he offered. "Thanks." As I took a sip, I felt his assessing eyes on me. I didn't look away, but damn if I didn't sense he knew exactly how much I wanted Jade.

If I was wondering about it, he clarified immediately. "Be careful. Jade doesn't date, and Lucas will be plenty pissed if he thinks you're after Jade for just a little fun."

"I'm not after anyone for just a little fun." My words came out sharp, and I knew I sounded defensive.

Jackson leaned his hips against the counter as he took a slow sip of his coffee. "Okay then. I guess you might wanna be careful how you look at Jade then," he replied with a chuckle.

"What the hell does that mean?" I countered.

"It means you look at her like you'd like her for dinner. And before you go thinking I'm policing your sex life or love life, or what-the-hell ever, I'm not. I'm just giving you a little background."

"While we're on the subject, what's the story behind Jade not dating?"

Jackson chuckled again. "For someone who's not curious, you sure are curious."

"Oh, for fuck's sake, I am curious," I admitted, surprising myself. I trusted Jackson and knew he wasn't one to talk, so I figured I might as well ask.

Jackson eyed me for a long beat, but then shrugged. "Some shit went down when she was in college. I don't have all the details, but I do know a good friend of hers, a guy, spiked her drink with one of those date rape drugs."

Anger slashed through me, burning hot and then icy cold, the kind of cold that stings. I lowered my mug before I'd almost taken a sip. "A friend of hers raped her?" My words were low and laced with fury.

"Pump the brakes, man. No. At least, not that I'm aware of. They were just hanging out at a bar, and one of the waitresses saw him spike her drink when Jade went to the bathroom. He was arrested at the bar. So, nothing happened, but

Lucas says she hasn't dated since. She's pretty open that she's not interested in dating. That's all I know."

"Do you know who the friend was?"

Jackson took another sip of coffee before he replied, "I can't recall. I don't think it's going to do you a damned bit of good to go down that road. I don't think Jade will appreciate it. Especially from some guy who's supposedly not interested." His gaze held a knowing glint.

I forced myself to take a deep breath, letting it out slowly. Although I was still fucking furious, there wasn't a single thing I could do about what happened to Jade. Not now and maybe not ever. "Fair enough," I finally replied.

Jackson gave me another assessing look before he dipped his head in a nod. "You're a good man, Walker. I may not have known you all that long, but I know that. Proceed with caution is the only advice I have."

Chapter Seventeen

JADE

I felt a bead of sweat roll down between my breasts. Restless, I reached for the glass of ice water Dani had just handed me and took several gulps. I hoped, rather pointlessly, that no one could see how flushed I was. Considering how hot my cheeks were, I prayed no one was paying attention. It was crowded at the table, and I was seated between Walker and Valentina.

It was all Valentina's fault that I was here to begin with. My soon to be sister-in-law had invited me to have dinner and drinks with "the girls." Ever since Valentina moved in with Lucas, she'd become a dear friend. Which was awesome because I loved my brother and my niece. It would have been mighty inconvenient, and it might've possibly come to blows, if my older brother had fallen for a woman I didn't like.

Not that I had a right to dictate what happened in my brother's love life, but I sure thought I did. Valentina hadn't been aware this wasn't just a girls' dinner. She'd thought the guys were going out to the bar. Instead, the guys, including

Walker, decided to grab dinner at the lodge before heading out to the bar.

As it was, now I was stuck with Walker practically plastered to one side of my body because the bench was crowded. That was definitely a minus to the whole bench seating option. When there were actual chairs, people could only get so close.

"Oh sorry!" Valentina said, her red curls bouncing when she faced my way. She cast an apologetic smile after elbowing me in the shoulder while she was attempting to serve herself from a platter of herbed roasted potatoes.

"No problem," I replied. "I'm sure I'll return the favor."

Walker's knee shifted, nudging my thigh. That subtle touch sent fire licking up my leg. "Sorry."

His low, sexy drawl set my body alight. My belly did a slow flip with flutters spinning inside. I took another gulp of my ice water before replying, "Just like I told Valentina, I'm sure I'll return the favor." In Walker's case, I couldn't resist nudging my knee against his thigh.

"That didn't seem like an accident," he murmured, low enough that no one else could hear.

Considering the murmur of voices around us and how many people were talking, it was unlikely anyone would notice if we had a semi-private conversation. Minus the actual expectation of privacy, of course.

Beyond Valentina and Lucas, we were surrounded by other couples. Dani and Wade, Shay and Jackson, and Dawson and Evie. In fact, the only single people at the table were myself, Walker, and Skylar, the vet tech. I told myself it was a relief not to be the only single person at the table. Of course, Walker's presence beside me had me so stirred up, I could barely think.

I resisted the urge to lift my ice-cold glass and rub it over my neck. Instead, I served myself some food and unintentionally bumped Valentina with one elbow and Walker with the other.

"Proving your point?" Walker teased.

This time, I gave in to the urge to look his way. Major mistake. The moment I met his eyes and saw the heat banked in his gaze, my stomach spun, and another wash of heat rolled through my body.

"No, it's just crowded." I forced myself to look away.

"So how is Dave?" Dani asked Walker.

Walker looked over. "He's doing okay."

"Can't believe the guy had a heart attack on his wedding night," Dawson offered in between bites.

"What exactly happened? I haven't had a chance to ask," Jackson chimed in.

Dawson replied, "Dave had a heart attack right after the reception."

"Damn." Jackson's gaze swung to Walker. "So he's okay?"

"Oh yeah. Now he's gotta get used to eating healthier," Walker said with a wry smile.

"We never did hear how your fake date went," Dawson interjected.

"Clearly, I'm not up to speed on anything. What the hell is a fake date?" Shay asked.

I felt Valentina elbow me, and I returned the favor.

Dawson grinned. "Walker needed a date, so Jade went to keep his old girlfriend off his back."

"Well? Did it work?" Dani asked, arching a brow.

Jesus. Now, this was a group conversation. I knew avoiding it would only raise more suspicions, so I shrugged. Everyone knew, so there was no sense in not talking about it. But everyone didn't know that our date turned out not so fake after all. If you counted that we knew each other quite intimately now.

Walker finished chewing and took a sip of water before responding, "It went well. I mean, the whole weekend was overshadowed by Dave's heart attack. Jade was convincing."

I smiled. "I can be charming when I choose."

Valentina grinned. "You're always charming."

"Not always," I murmured in reply before draining the rest of my water.

"Huh? A fake date. At least now I'm up to speed on the gossip," Shay said.

"It's not gossip," I retorted, perhaps a bit too sharply.

When I turned, I caught Dani watching me, a clear speculative gleam in her eyes.

———

A few hours later, the guys had left to go to the bar as planned. It was just the girls—the girls being me, Valentina, Shay, Dani, Evie and Grace. I had to put up with more curiosity than I preferred.

"What's with all the questions?" I muttered on the heels of Dani asking me again about the weekend with Walker.

Dani lifted her wine glass and wrinkled her nose as she spun it in her fingers. "There're always questions. Especially when someone looks at a guy the way you were looking at Walker tonight," she said pointedly.

"This from you who took forever to admit you never fell out of love with Wade," I retorted.

Dani blew a puff of air out of her lips, directing it toward a loose curl falling over her eye and expertly sending it up in the air and out of her eyes. "And I finally got around to it. So there," she said firmly.

"I feel like I'm at a disadvantage." I cast a pleading look in Valentina's direction. But, damn her, she was replying to a text on her phone, probably from my brother.

"What do you mean?" Grace interjected.

"I don't work here all the time like the rest of you."

Valentina finally set her phone down. Her cheeks were pink, further proof that she was texting with Lucas. "It doesn't matter. It's quality, not quantity," she teased.

I sighed. "I had a very nice time at the wedding. Well, except for Dave's heart attack."

"I wasn't asking about the wedding, I was asking what you thought about Walker," Dani returned.

"Are you telling me you don't think Walker's handsome? Because I don't have a thing for him or anything, but that guy is like seriously hot," Shay offered.

Valentina snorted a laugh, finally coming to my defense. "Jade just said they had a nice time at the wedding. Let's leave it alone."

Dani threw a knowing look my way, but shifted topics, turning her lasered curiosity to Evie. "Speaking of men, when is Mack moving home? It seems like he's changed plans several times," Dani commented, referring to Evie's older brother.

Evie shrugged. "He has. When I talked to him last week, he said no matter what, he'd be home this summer."

Shay piped up, "Jackson said he told Mack about the upcoming opening on the first responder crew here with one of the guys moving."

"Did you want some wine?" Valentina asked from my side as she filled her glass.

I shook my head. "No, thanks. I'm driving, so I'll stick with water," I replied.

Fortunately for me, the conversation didn't loop back to me. It wasn't much later that I was driving home through the early summer darkness. The mountain air was glorious this time of year. There was just a hint of the humidity to come, and the nights were still cool. With the windows rolled down as I drove home, the air caressed my skin. It was laden with the scents of rich greenery and flowers in bloom. With the half-moon low in the sky and illuminating a mountain ridge in the distance, the night felt a bit magical.

I paused to pull off the road at a small lookout. Climbing out of my car, I walked across the small parking area to sit on a bench. During the daytime, this spot offered a lovely view of Stolen Hearts Valley. The quiet seeped into me, and

I savored the low sounds of crickets chirping in the darkness and the trees rustling in the breeze.

Leaning my head back, I looked up into the velvety dark sky with stars scattered across and glittering in the night. I took a deep breath, the tension bundled inside ever since I'd seen Walker earlier tonight finally starting to ease slightly.

I couldn't quite believe how far I'd let things go with him that weekend. I'd almost convinced myself in the intervening two weeks that it was just a fluke, that when I saw him again it would feel normal. Maybe there would be a little buzz of chemistry, but nothing more. I was so wrong, so spectacularly wrong. At least I knew my judgment wasn't the greatest when it came to men.

Every time I thought about how hard it was for me to trust, I thought about Shay and what she'd been through, and I felt ridiculous. She'd suffered public humiliation and a brutal physical assault. Yet, she'd walked through that fire and was now deeply in love with Jackson. Whenever I tried to tell myself I could find that same courage to trust again, I bumped into so many doubts.

I closed my eyes and took a slow breath. A friend for years had slipped a date rape drug in my drink. I would always wonder what he'd intended to do. Thanks to a waitress looking in the direction of our table when I went to the restroom, nothing happened. I would never know what he intended to do.

Trust was so fucking hard to come by in my mind. It had been so easy to tell myself I would never date, that I would never be interested in anyone. I hadn't considered it worth the trouble.

Enter Walker and me agreeing to that stupid wedding and thinking it was no big deal. Now, not a single night passed when I didn't dream about him. I hated admitting I brought myself to climax more than once with thoughts of his gaze locked on mine when he took me to the brink and beyond.

I was snapped out of my restless train of thought at the sound of a car approaching on the road, followed by a loud thump and a squeak. I jumped up and hurried back toward the edge of the winding highway. I watched the taillights disappearing in the darkness.

I knew I'd likely heard an animal get hit. My heart was pounding in my chest, and I felt sick. I fumbled for my phone in my pocket. I tapped the button for the flashlight and searched around carefully. Scanning the road, I saw a small shape in the darkness. It appeared to be a young opossum. It was still alive, moving slowly as it dragged itself to the side of the road.

Fortunately, it was coming in my direction and stopped once it had reached the small parking area where my car was. I wasn't stupid, so I approached it carefully.

"Hey, sweetie," I said softly as I stopped a few feet away.

The little opossum with its worried face turned in my direction. I could see its rapid breath, rising and falling, its entire small body moving with it. Stepping closer, I moved the flashlight over it carefully, ascertaining that one of its legs was badly injured.

I sprang into action. "Hang on, I'm going to get you in a little sling and we're gonna take you to Jackson's office," I said conversationally as if the opossum was going to answer.

After digging through the back of my car, I came out with a blanket and a leash. The leash was left over from a friend's dog I'd dog sat a few months back and never gotten around to returning the leash.

I was standing a few feet away, eyeing the opossum in the darkness as I attempted to sort out how to handle the situation. I heard the sound of another vehicle rounding the bend in the road and hoped that no one bothered to stop. If they did, they would probably think I was crazy.

I considered calling Jackson and Shay because I'd be calling them anyway. Maybe Jackson could tell me how to safely gather up this little guy. When I heard the sound of the wheels getting closer, I noticed a truck slowing and pulling in behind my car.

"Great," I muttered to myself. "Here's hoping whoever this is doesn't think I'm insane, or it's not some asshole."

"Jade?"

When I recognized Walker's voice, I instantly felt my cheeks get hot.

Chapter Eighteen

WALKER

Jade stood on the side of the winding highway in a small viewing area with what appeared to be a dog leash and a blanket in her hand. An opossum was on the ground a few feet in front of her. As I approached this rather unexpected scene, I had to fight back the urge to laugh.

"Now, why doesn't it surprise me that it looks like you're planning to wrap that injured opossum in a blanket?" I asked when I reached Jade's side.

I could see the flush on her cheeks from the glare of the headlights I'd left on.

"Well, it shouldn't surprise you," she retorted, resting the hand holding the leash on her hip. "He's injured. I'm going to get him in my car and call Jackson and take him down to the clinic."

I almost sighed, but I caught myself. Jade was going to do this whether I thought it was a good idea or not. I might as well be helpful.

I knew a bit about wild animal rescue because it was something my mom did on the side. Her expertise was birds, but nonetheless. "Can I help?"

Jade's eyes widened and then a smile broke out. Her smile was like a lasso cinching around my heart. "You'll help? Really?"

Taking a breath, I nodded, ignoring the almost rib-cracking kick of my heart. "You call Jackson, and I'll get this little guy wrapped up in the blanket."

Jade promptly handed over the dog leash and the blanket. She had her phone out and was calling Jackson as I approached the opossum. The opossum was indeed a male because I could see there was no pouch, but I didn't know if Jade hadn't gotten close enough to confirm earlier.

With a little care and some quick work, I had him rolled in the blanket. He wasn't too thrilled with the state of affairs and snarled at me, but I had him in the blanket before he had a chance to bite me.

"What'd Jackson say?" I asked after I had deposited the opossum into the back of my truck and closed the window to the truck cover.

Jade eyed my truck in the darkness. "Are you sure we should leave him back there?"

"Yes," I said firmly. "As it is, I don't have a crate and he could easily get out. This way, he'll be in the back of my truck and not in the backseat of your car."

Jade opened her mouth—I presumed to argue with me—but then snapped it shut with a sigh. "I guess you're right. Jackson said he'll meet us at the clinic. Can I just ride with you?"

I lifted my phone, tapping the screen to see the time. "We're closer than he is because he was still at Lost Deer Bar when I left. I don't think it's wise for you to leave your car here. We're about a mile away from your place. I'll follow you over, and you can ride with me from there. How's that sound?"

Jade nodded quickly. "Perfect." Without waiting, she hurried to her car, calling over her shoulder, "Just follow me."

As if I didn't know where she lived, right down the road from me.

Only a few minutes later, Jade was jumping into the passenger seat of my truck. "Thank you so much, Walker," she said as she buckled her seat belt. "I just want the opossum to be okay."

"I think he'll be okay. Honestly, considering that someone hit him, he's pretty damn lucky. It looks like he injured one of his back legs."

"That's what I thought." Jade was practically vibrating beside me. She kept peeking into the back of the truck after asking me if she could open up a small window between the front and the back.

After we arrived at the clinic, we found Skylar already there along with Shay. Jackson was washing up in the back. Between Skylar and Shay, we got the opossum into a carrier to bring him inside and Skylar promptly gave him a sedative.

Jackson examined the opossum and confirmed he had a broken hind leg. Jade insisted on waiting until Jackson confirmed there were no internal injuries and he'd set the broken leg. Jade only agreed to leave after he assured her the opossum was going to be fine, and he and Shay would make sure he was comfortable for the night.

The space inside my truck was quiet as I drove through the darkness toward home. I'd come to discover it was impossible to be near Jade and not feel that crackle of electricity between us. However, during the opossum rescue, I'd been understandably preoccupied. Now that was over, it felt as if the air around us was shimmering and vibrating with the desire banked inside my body.

Moonlight fell through the window, casting her profile partially in shadow. Her face had clean lines with a slightly stubborn tilt to her jaw. All of it was softened by her full, lush lips. As if she sensed my gaze on her, she turned, her eyes catching with mine. It felt as if a flame flickered to life between us.

I had to look away—I was driving, after all—but I had to force it. This thing with Jade, whatever it was, was powerful, its own force to reckon with. Although it was unsettling, I wanted her fiercely and with a need that should have given me pause.

When I pulled into her driveway, I faced her. "I'll walk you in." When I cut the engine, the air was heavy, laden with raw, charged electricity. The power of it was burgeoning with each passing second.

I didn't wait for Jade's reply, climbing out quickly and rounding the truck to get her door. She was already opening it and cut me a sharp look as I held it.

"I do have manners," I murmured.

Her laugh in return was throaty, the sound of it tossing more fuel on the flames kindling between us. When we stepped onto the small landing in front of her door, Jade turned to me.

I decided not to bother playing this any way other than blunt. "I want you."

Her breath came out in a startled puff and then she laughed again. "Well, just get right to the point, why don't you?"

"Thought it might make it easier."

I waited, giving her a clear chance to send me packing. There was a small light under the curved enclosure above the landing. Her green eyes glittered underneath it, and her cheeks were tinged pink.

"Okay," she said simply, before turning and unlocking her door. She held it open for me to follow her inside.

My gaze scanned the space. I couldn't help myself, my curiosity for Jade continued to grow. Just now, I took in that she had gauzy gray curtains in her windows, with touches of purple accents around the room. A half-wall served as a divider between the living room and kitchen and was painted in a deep purple, while the rest of the walls were soft

cream. There were hardwood floors with round rugs strategi-
cally placed.

The living room had a large sectional sofa in the corner
and a cushioned ottoman. Aside from a television mounted
on the wall and two end tables, that was the extent of the
furnishings. The kitchen, to the left from the front door, had
a round table and counters lining three walls. The space was
cozy, although I would've expected as much given the size of
the house.

Jade kicked off her shoes and shrugged out of her jacket,
hanging it on a coat stand that looked like a flower. The
space, though simple, was a touch more whimsical than I
would've expected for Jade.

She tossed her purse on the table by the door. "Well, are
you coming in?"

I felt my lips kick up into a smile. "I'm already inside."

"I guess you can stay there. Would you like something to
drink?" she called over her shoulder as she strode away.

My eyes immediately were drawn to the subtle sway of
her hips and the swing of her hair. I didn't know if it was the
husky edge to her voice, or that I thought earlier about
wrapping her long glossy hair in my hand as I fucked her
from behind, but I was galvanized into motion. I didn't have
a jacket on, but I quickly toed off my boots and followed her.

I caught her hand just as she was walking past the half-
wall and into the kitchen. When she spun back, she bumped
against me. I felt the sudden press of my cock against the
zipper of my jeans.

"No."

Her eyes widened slightly, and her lips parted. "No,
what?"

"I don't want something to drink. I told you what I want.
You."

Lust was tightening screws in every corner of my body. I
could see the wild flutter of Jade's pulse at the base of her

throat and held back the urge to lean down and taste the sweet, sensitive skin there.

"What are we doing, Walker?" Her words were just above a whisper.

Jade, who was so strong and so guarded with that sharp edge, had a hint of vulnerability flickering in her eyes. The lasso she'd tossed around my heart hours ago, when we stood beside the road and I asked if she wanted my help, tightened.

Jade was sexy, beautiful, strong, and standoffish. That she would even let her guard down enough to let the vulnerability shine through, no matter how hard she tried to hide it, took my breath away.

"I don't know if I can answer that."

My reply was honest because I didn't know what else to say. Stepping closer, I lifted a hand, tucking a loose lock of her hair behind her ear and letting my fingers trail through the silky strands. "All I know is we have unfinished business. But, I'll leave. Right now. If that's what you want. Is that what you want?"

I could feel every beat of my heart reverberating inside my body as I waited for her to respond. She shook her head, just barely.

"Is that a 'no, you don't want me,' or 'no, you don't want me to leave'?" I prompted.

Jade's cheeks turned an even deeper shade of pink as she cocked her head to the side. "Oh, for God's sake. You're gonna make me say it, aren't you?"

I nodded and waited.

After too many beats of my heart, she replied, "Please stay."

Chapter Nineteen

WALKER

The moment that single word crossed her lips—stay—it felt as if hot sparks filled the air, electricity reverberating around us.

Jade's tongue darted out, the pink tip swiping at one corner of her mouth. My restraint snapped its frayed tether. Stepping closer, I slid a hand around to cup her nape. My heartbeat thundered through my entire body, each beat a strike against the flint of desire between us.

She moved closer just as I did, her warm, soft curves pressing against me. The moment was a strange mix of slow and fast. The urgency of lust driving me contrasted with the way everything felt suspended in a haze of sensation.

Bending low, I brushed my lips across hers, and it felt as if sparks struck at the point of contact. Jade made a little sound, something between a whimper and a hitch of her breath at the back of her throat. At the sound, I fit my mouth over hers and dove into the fire with her.

Jade was no passive kisser. The moment she threw herself into it, our tongues were tangling in a sensual war. Our kiss went spiraling into madness—hot, wet, and intense.

With one hand tangling in her glossy locks, I slipped my other down her spine to cup her bottom, pulling her against my arousal.

I was so hard, the pressure of it was an ache, one I knew would not be relieved until I was buried inside of Jade. Nothing else would slake the ferocity of my need. It was a need like no other, quite specific. *All* I needed was Jade, and I needed *all* of Jade.

When she shifted and we bumped into the side of the counter, I turned and lifted her, sliding her hips onto the counter. Our kiss never broke.

At this point, I was all but breathing through our kiss. She was as frantic as me, curling her legs around my hips and tugging me into the cradle of hers. The hard ridge of my arousal pressed against the heat of her core. She let out another one of those moans into my mouth before breaking free and gulping in air. After a few ragged breaths, I let my gaze drift over her. Her eyes were heavy-lidded, her cheeks flushed, and her lips swollen and pink.

She wore this silky camisole underneath an open blouse. I could see the taut peaks of her nipples pressing against the silk. I lifted a hand, lightly cupping a breast and letting my thumb tease back and forth.

Jade's tongue swiped across her bottom lip when her mouth parted, and she let out a soft sigh. I could appreciate the sight of a beautiful woman aroused, but no woman had ever gotten to me the way Jade did.

Simply watching her sent need licking like flames through me. I was on fire. For her.

She rocked her hips into me. Although I didn't think it was quite possible, a surge of blood shot to my groin, swelling my cock even more. As I squeezed a nipple between my fingers, satisfaction sizzled through me when she arched into my touch and let out a low moan.

"You're killin' me," I murmured.

Her eyes had fallen closed and they opened, piercing me

with a sharp, blazing hot look. She leaned forward, stringing fiery kisses along my collarbone. Reaching between us, she made quick work of the buttons on my fly and freed my cock. She slid her palm up and down my swollen, aching arousal.

"You have too many clothes on," she murmured when I let out a rough groan.

"Same to you, sweetheart."

I pushed her blouse off her shoulders. In a few seconds, my shirt joined her blouse and camisole on the floor, and she sat before me in a cream silk bra. Her dusty pink nipples were dark. Bending down, I closed my mouth over one, sucking straight through the silk and savoring her sharp cry when I did the same to the other.

Everything with Jade was a battle inside. I wanted to rush through this to relieve the intense need driving me. That urge wrestled with the deep, aching need to savor every second. When I lifted my head, she trailed one hand over the planes of my chest before reaching between us with her thumb and flicking her bra open. Her plump breasts were bare to me, her nipples damp.

Before I could think, she was curling her hand around my cock again as she blazed a trail of kisses across my chest and dipped her head down to swipe the drop of the pre-cum on the tip. With lust rushing through me like a river in spring, I lifted her against me. I thought we were in agreement that we needed more clothes off and growled against the side of her neck. Holding her up with an arm, I tugged at her leggings, only setting her down long enough to shove them down over her hips along with her panties.

Demonstrating just how in agreement we were, Jade kicked her feet free. Then, I lifted her again as her legs curled around my hips and her slick core kissed the head of my cock when she rocked against me. I was barely hanging on to any semblance of control. I was beyond relieved I still had my jeans on even if they were only hanging around my hips. Sliding her hips back onto the counter, I reached into my back pocket, tugging my wallet loose and yanking out the condom I kept there for emergencies.

I hadn't had anything resembling an emergency in years. But, Jade had been an emergency ever since I'd let myself get close to her. My need to be as physically close to her as possible transcended the concept of need. It was bone-deep, primitive, and raw.

In a matter of seconds, I'd rolled the condom on and was shifting my hands to grip her hips, savoring the give of her flesh under my grip. "Now would be the time to tell me no." I gasped.

She sat before me on the counter with her nipples playing peekaboo through the dark locks of hair falling over her shoulders. I could feel the heat of her calling to me, but I held still. When I let my gaze wander down, the sight of her glistening pink pussy nearly undid me.

I dragged my eyes to hers. She took a breath and lifted her chin. "Didn't I already make it clear what I wanted?"

"Maybe you should tell me exactly what you want."

Jade's feisty, bossy edge had me rising to meet her and push her just a little further.

"I want you inside of me. Now," she ordered. She curled her legs around my hips and arched into me, rocking and sliding her slick folds along the underside of my cock.

On the heels of a deep breath, I adjusted the angle of my hips and sank home into the heart of her. My forehead fell to hers as her snug channel pulsed around me when I buried myself balls deep.

If I tried to convince myself this was just about sex, the moment I was physically joined with her, the fusion was an echo through every fiber of my being. When I opened my eyes, mere inches from hers, I felt the look in her eyes in my heart. My own heart gave a resounding kick in response.

Chapter Twenty

JADE

With the feeling of Walker stretching me and filling me so exquisitely perfect, I opened my eyes and found his gaze. Right there. His eyes instantly captured mine, and it felt as if a force field was pulling me in. I could hardly bear the intimacy of it.

We held still for several echoing beats of my heart. He drew back slowly, oh-so-slowly, before sinking inside once again. My body was restless, rocking into him and desperate for every time he filled and stretched me.

Although we were in my kitchen on the counter, and everything about the situation screamed it was a casual, rushed fuck, it felt anything but. With Walker's palms gripping my hips, he set the pace. His forehead rested against mine, and my breasts were pressed against his hard muscled chest.

Each moment blurred into the next. All I knew was the feel of him inside of me with his arms holding me close. Pleasure was gathering in my core, tighter and tighter, fire feeding into itself with each stroke of his hips into mine. I chased my release, bursts of pleasure scattering through me, each one more intense than the last. The angle of our joining was such that every time he sank into me, he brushed against my clit, just enough to drive me wild and not quite enough to push me over into my sweet release.

He brushed his lips against mine, and I murmured his name like a plea.

"All you had to do was ask," he growled against my lips just as he reached between us to tease his fingers over my clit.

Everything pulled tight inside, and then broke loose, pleasure bursting through me as I cried out and my channel clenched around his cock. While my body was still rippling with the aftershocks of my climax, he surged deeply once more. I felt him go tight as a bow against me before he murmured my name against my lips and shuddered into me.

We stayed like that as my head finally fell forward, nestling into the curve of his neck while I tried to catch my breath. I didn't want to move. Ever. This felt too good. It was an escape like no other. I forgot everything for a few moments, even that old promise I'd made to never let any man make me lose myself.

When I became aware of how deeply I'd let go, I remembered. That promise had nothing to do with pleasure. It was simply that I viewed losing myself this completely as a sign that I trusted myself with a man. I simply hadn't believed that was possible.

I honestly didn't know how, but somehow Walker smoothed the sharp edges of my anxiety threatening to cut into the moment. He brushed my hair away from my face. When I thought he might insist that we talk, he didn't, at least not about anything of weight. He pressed a kiss to my temple and slowly untangled himself from the cage of my legs before asking casually where the bathroom was.

By the time he returned to the kitchen, I had gotten my leggings and camisole back on. When he caught my eyes, a smile hitched up one corner of his mouth. "Oh, now, that's a disappointment."

I bit my lip as I smiled and asked, "What?"

"I thought we were in agreement on the amount of clothes we were wearing. I still don't have my shirt on."

I burst out laughing. His gaze sobered as he stepped closer, reaching down to scoop my blouse from the floor. "But you're cold, so I won't insist." When his palm caressed my shoulder and down my arm and I felt the goose bumps under his warm touch, my heart nearly tripped and fell over.

He had lightened the moment perfectly. While I knew I would obsess later—for hours probably—about what had passed between us in that heady, intense passion, right now, I asked him if he wanted a drink.

When he said yes, I didn't plan on enjoying a glass of wine with him while we sat at my kitchen table talking about nothing and everything. I certainly didn't plan on getting sleepy enough that my chin fell to my chest. I came half awake when he lifted me into his arms. I most certainly didn't plan on letting him carry me to bed. And then, when he moved to leave the room, I didn't plan on reaching out to catch his hand in mine. I certainly didn't plan on saying, "Stay."

Chapter Twenty-One

JADE

"I swear, he's fine," Shay said, looking at me from behind the reception desk at the vet clinic.

"Can I see him?" I asked in return.

She grinned, her blond ponytail swinging when she held up a finger and grabbed the ringing phone. "Stolen Hearts Vet Clinic," she said as she lifted it to her ear.

I wandered away from the desk, walking across the waiting area to look at a bulletin board on the wall. It was covered in thank you cards, along with many photographs from various animals that either came to the vet clinic, or were part of the rescue program they ran.

While Shay scheduled an appointment for whoever was on the phone, I heard the front door to the clinic open and reflexively glanced over my shoulder to see Walker coming in. He hadn't seen me yet, so I took a moment to absorb the sight of him.

My pulse sped up and my belly did a quick little flip. He wore faded blue jeans and battered leather boots. A black T-shirt that did nothing to hide his muscled frame topped off his look. Damn, that man did a T-shirt and jeans amazingly well. He was mouth-watering—all rangy muscle as he moved with easy grace toward the reception desk.

His name slipped out of my mouth without my permission. His feet stopped and he turned, his silver-smoke gaze locking with mine instantly. I swear it felt like a little flame flickered through the air between us. The moment was electric. It had only been a few hours since I'd seen him, and I was already a puddle of need.

I'd woken this morning with his arms wrapped around me after sleeping better than I had in years. After several thrashing beats of my heart, Walker angled across the room to where I stood off to the side of the reception desk. Shay's gaze was curious when her eyes bounced between Walker and me.

"Hey." That one word, spoken in Walker's gravelly drawl, set butterflies alight in my belly.

I took a shallow breath because my lungs couldn't do anything else. "Hey. What are you doing here?"

Just then, the door to the clinic opened again. This time, my older brother came through. Lucas's eyes bounced to us instantly.

Just what I need. My protective brother as an audience.

If Walker thought anything of Lucas's presence, he didn't let it show. His eyes held mine a bit too long for comfort, and I found I couldn't look away. The electricity shimmering around us felt so powerful I irrationally worried my brother could actually see it.

Now, you know you're losing your mind, my inner critic quickly chided me.

"Checking on the opossum?" Lucas asked as he stopped beside Walker and me.

"How did you hear about the opossum?" I countered.

"I told him," Walker replied with a slow grin that sent those butterflies completely wild in my belly. It was enough to try to manage my body's crazy reaction to Walker on my own. It was far more unsettling with an audience, especially one that might have an opinion.

"We do work together, in case you forgot," Lucas said with a pointed look in my direction. "I'm glad you didn't try to wrangle a wild, injured opossum on your own, by the way."

Defensiveness flashed inside, and I put my hands on my hips, narrowing my eyes at my brother. "I'm sure I could've handled it fine. I do appreciate Walker's help, though."

"Injured wild animals are not something to fuck around with, Jade. At least Walker has some experience because his mom used to have a bird rehab program," Lucas replied.

"She did?" My eyes swung to Walker.

Somehow during the course of events last night, that detail did not come up. I was hungry for every little detail I could absorb about Walker. That little detail about me—my greedy curiosity about all things Walker—should've sent me running.

Walker nodded. "Yep. She didn't have a rescue like the one here, but she got trained to rehab wild birds. She still does it here and there." He glanced over his shoulder toward Shay when she hung up the phone. "Any updates?"

Shay came around from behind the reception desk. I stepped over toward her, both disappointed and relieved to create some distance from Walker. That man was an actual magnet for me. I needed to get myself in hand.

"How is he?" I asked when I reached Shay's side and rested my elbow on the counter surrounding the reception desk.

"He's fine," she said with a smile. "He had a broken leg, so Jackson set it last night and put a good brace on. He's all settled over in the rescue barn today."

Relief washed through me. "Good. So what happens now? Will he be able to be released into the wild?"

"It depends."

"Depends on what?" I pressed.

Walker stepped closer, and my pulse instantly picked up its pace. I hoped like hell my skin wasn't flushed because I could feel heat suffusing me. I could honestly say I'd never experienced the concept of hot and bothered until I met Walker. Now, it seemed to be a regular state of affairs for my body when he happened to be around.

I heard Jackson before I saw him. "On how well his recovery goes," Jackson's voice said, preceding him before he came out of the hallway into the reception area.

"What do you mean?" I asked when he stopped beside Shay and leaned over to dust a kiss over her lips. I swear, they were too sweet. It almost hurt my heart a little. I'd never envied their connection until right this second.

Longing pierced me—a deep wish to have someone look at me the way Jackson looked at Shay, a longing to be able to trust someone like that. Shay had plenty of reasons not to trust, but there wasn't even a hint of doubt when I saw her look at Jackson.

I kicked those feelings away. I couldn't hope for something like that and was startled to even wish I could.

Jackson lifted his head and belatedly replied to my question when I impatiently tapped the toe of my cowboy boot against the desk. "Well, it was a pretty bad break and his hips were banged up. We're not gonna know for a few weeks just how good his mobility will be. He needs to be able to fend for himself out there. Some animals rehab easier than others. The downside to opossums is they're easily domesticated. This guy is quite young. I'd guess him to be less than a year old."

I reflexively looked toward Walker, as if somehow he could reassure me. As soon as my eyes met his, it felt as if something struck me right in my solar plexus. This was crazy, really crazy.

"That's how these things go," Lucas said from my side. "No matter what, he survived, probably thanks to you."

My brother knew me well enough to sense I was upset

and unsettled. I prayed he had no idea it wasn't just over the opossum. Walker blessedly stayed quiet, although I felt his gaze on me when Lucas looked away to say something to Jackson.

"Can I go see him?" I asked Shay.

"Of course. He's in the recovery area in the rescue barn. It's not in the main section, but in the room at the back," she explained.

"Do I need anyone to come with me?"

Jackson interjected, "No, but just looking."

"Got it. I just want to see him."

"Mind if I tag along?" Walker asked

"Fine with me. You helped me get him here, so of course."

Lucas chimed in, "I gotta roll. When I saw your car here, I stopped to ask if you could babysit Rylie tomorrow."

"Of course."

"I know you always say that, but it's not your full-time job anymore now that she goes to school. I never want to assume," Lucas replied.

I leveled my brother with a glare. "Assume all you want when it comes to my niece. If I ever have plans, I'll happily change them."

Lucas grinned. "Still going to ask, and thanks. I have my physical tomorrow, and Valentina and I are doing a shopping run in Asheville. Text her tonight if you need anything."

"Text Valentina, not you?" I asked as he turned away.

Lucas looked back with a sheepish smile. "She's more organized than me."

"I bet," I called as he waved. "Okay if I get there by nine?"

"Perfect." The clinic's door swung shut behind him, muffling his reply.

Relieved Lucas had left, I turned to Walker. "All right, let's go check on our little friend." Looking back at Shay, I asked, "Have you named him yet?"

Jackson laughed along with Walker. "Since y'all found him, I guess you can do the honors."

"Let's go see him and we'll decide," I said to Walker.

"Before you go, wanna grab drinks tonight with Valentina and me?" Shay asked.

"I'd love to. Text me?" At Shay's nod, I turned to go.

Chapter Twenty-Two

JADE

Walker was quiet as we walked outside, crossing the gravel parking lot between the clinic and the old farmhouse where Jackson and Shay lived. We ducked through the fence into the horse pasture. As we made our way through the pasture, Mischief, Shay's favorite pony, trotted over to greet us. Mischief was a friendly and mischievous Banker pony, rescued from the Outer Banks after his mother almost died when he was a colt.

A dark bay with three white socks and a white star on his face, Mischief flicked his tail as he slowed to a walk and stopped beside us. Walker reached up, casually scratching him behind the ears. "Hey, buddy. How ya doing?" he asked conversationally.

Mischief answered by lifting his nose and sniffing Walker's shoulder before turning his attention to me. He sniffed when I held out my hand. I smoothed my palm down the side of his neck before we continued walking.

"You seem pretty comfortable around horses," I observed.

Walker lifted his shoulder in an easy shrug. "Yeah. Spent time around them growing up. How about you?"

"Same. Jackson's younger sister, Ash, was a friend growing up. She's not here right now, but I used to ride with her sometimes when we were kids."

At that moment, Mischief, who'd been ambling along beside us, nudged my shoulder with his nose, just barely knocking me off balance, but enough that I stumbled into Walker. He caught me around the waist, steadying me. The moment happened quickly. In a second, I was looking up into his eyes with the feel of his strong muscled arm around my waist. All I wanted was to kiss him.

I saw the answering flare of desire in his eyes. Heat blasted through me and my channel clenched. That was how bad I had it for this man. One look into his eyes and nothing more sent my mind spinning down the track where all I could think about was the delicious feel of him inside of me.

The sound of Mischief swishing his tail nudged me back into sanity. I recalled we were standing in full view of anyone over by the vet clinic and farmhouse. Stepping back hurriedly, I licked my lips and took a breath. "Thank you."

Walker simply nodded, and we began walking again. The rescue barn was on the far side of the horse pasture. We went through another paddock, and Walker slid open the main door into the barn.

I was instantly distracted by Squeaky, a cute mini pig who—you guessed it—squeaked. Her little curly tail wiggled as she came over and sniffed my ankle with her nose. I knelt down beside her, stroking down her back the way she liked. "Hey, Squeaky. Where's Gloria?" I asked.

Gloria was the farm's other pig. She was anything but mini. Although, that was how she ended up here. She had been bought as a pet for a family only to quickly outgrow her small stature. Although Squeaky couldn't exactly answer me, Gloria did for her. She ambled out of the stall they shared farther down the aisle. The large white and black pig approached me, making her usual snuffling sound.

Walker had closed the barn door behind us and leaned over to greet Gloria. "Hey, girl. Are you keeping an eye on the latest patient?"

Maybe it was silly, but my heart squeezed at the way Walker spoke to animals. He talked to them like they were his friends, and as if they might actually answer him in return.

For the rescue program, only the horses were kept over in the lower floor of the barn where the vet clinic was housed, which was built into a slope. This barn housed Gloria and Squeaky, a few goats, some chickens on the outside, and there was also a kennel for the dogs on the other side. Any of the other odds and ends of critters that landed here were usually in this barn.

Given that it was midday, most of the dogs were out in the fenced area of the kennel. I paused to pet an indeterminate breed dog who was wagging her tail like crazy. Walker was waiting for me by the door to the recovery room at the back. Not that I spent much time here, but with Lucas working here as well as Valentina, I knew my way around. I'd even helped Valentina with feedings at the rescue program one week when Shay and Jackson were out of town.

The recovery room here, as explained to me by Valentina, was for those animals who needed a little extra care and time to recover, but didn't need to be monitored around the clock at the vet clinic. Jackson had a daybed in one of the offices for when he needed to monitor any patients overnight.

"Ready?" Walker asked when I stopped beside him.

"Let's go."

I reached for the door handle, and he curled one of his hands over mine before I turned it. "Don't forget we're not supposed to pet him."

I opened my mouth to argue, but his lips curled in a

smile, understanding held in his eyes. "Injured animals are going to get to your heart. They do mine, so that warning was for both of us," he explained.

I smiled sheepishly. "I know."

We walked into the room with the door swinging shut softly behind us.

The unnamed opossum was in a small raised enclosure. The area was, of course, clean and sterile. There were blankets in a rounded pile in one corner. He appeared to be sleeping as we approached, but opened his eyes and lifted his face.

"Oh, he's so cute!" I exclaimed as I reached reflexively for Walker's hand and squeezed it.

The opossum had a bright blue cast on his rear leg. I could see where Jackson shaved off some hair with some stitching toward the top of the hip joint. I leaned against the railing surrounding his enclosure. "Hey, little guy. I really want to pet him," I said when the opossum limped over curiously.

Walker glanced down as I looked up. "I know, and Jackson said we can't," he reminded me. "He made it through surgery and it looks like he's going to make a full recovery. That's the best we can hope for. What should we name him?"

I stared down at him for a moment, answering with the first name that came to mind because it felt right. "Everett."

Walker's slow smile sent my belly into a flip. "Perfect." He watched the cute opossum. "Hey, Everett. Hope you're comfy here."

Walker stepped back, while I lingered, watching as the opossum nudged the water bowl nearby before leaning in to drink from it. Turning, I slipped my hands into the pockets of my jeans. Walker was leaning against the door.

Sweet hell. That man was too good-looking. The universe had been ridiculously generous with him. My eyes trailed up his muscled thighs encased in denim, snagging for a moment on the strip of tanned skin, revealed from where his thumb was hooked over a belt loop and slightly pulling the waistband of his jeans below his T-shirt. My mouth practically watered at the sight of the defined V that I knew led to incredible things.

Flustered, I yanked my eyes upward only to find his right there waiting for me, flashing silver and going dark and stormy.

"Can I see you tonight?" he asked.

His question startled me. Not that I could've guessed what I expected him to say, but definitely not that. I was tingling all over and felt as if little sparks were bouncing around inside me. I tried to take a steadying breath, but it wasn't much help. Breathing when Walker was anywhere in my vicinity didn't exactly work for me. I settled for a few sips of air and ignored the heat rising on my face.

"Sure." My reply startled me more than Walker's question because my thoughts hadn't formed. The word of assent just slipped out.

His slow, naughty smile made me bite my lip as I struggled to get a hold of my runaway pulse.

"Come 'ere," he murmured, his voice husky.

Because apparently I did whatever Walker said, I didn't even think before I crossed the room. When I was standing in front of him, he released his thumb from his belt loop and put two fingers in one of mine, tugging me close.

"Seems I can't get enough of you, Jade," he murmured as I felt the heat of his arousal pressing in the cradle of my hips.

The ache at the apex of my thighs throbbed. When I looked into Walker's eyes, the intensity there stole my breath as my heart nearly drummed its way out of my chest. I couldn't even speak, much less absorb the implications of Walker saying something like that. This wasn't supposed to be happening. Not to me. Not with us.

When I took a shuddery breath, I felt my achingly hard

nipples press against his chest. Walker lifted his hand and
laced his fingers in my hair. His hand slid down to cup my
cheek just before his thumb traced over my lips. His touch
was like fire.

And then, he was dipping his head, his voice low. "Just
one kiss."

His hand curled around the nape of my neck as he fit his
mouth over mine. If I'd learned only one thing since I'd
stumbled into this madness with Walker, it was that he could
kiss like no other. He instantly commanded my mouth, his
tongue sweeping in and laying claim.

I wasn't used to being overcome. There was no other way
to describe it. I was adrift on the desire crashing through me
as he devoured my mouth. At the same time, I savored the
way he pulled back and gently dropped hot kisses at each
corner of my mouth before diving back in.

The sharp bark of one of the dogs in the kennel barely
punctured the haze in my mind. When Walker pulled back
again, catching my bottom lip in his teeth with a sensuous
tug, I realized I was plastered against him. His knee had
slipped between my thighs, and I was rocking my hips over
it, piercing bursts of pleasure emanating from my core.

"I think they're in here," I heard a voice saying.

I started to scramble away, but Walker held me fast.
"Tonight?"

"I'm supposed to get drinks with Valentina and Shay," I
gasped when his knee pressed against my clit.

"Oh, that's right," he murmured.

"Walker," I pleaded in a whisper when I heard footsteps
approaching the door.

He released me, and it was only then that I remembered
he was actually leaning against the door.

"Call me after that." He pushed away from the door,
right when the doorknob turned.

I hadn't taken Walker for a tease, but I was quickly

learning I'd underestimated just about everything about Walker.

"Hey, how's our little guy?" Jackson asked as he stepped in the room. "Forgot I needed to give him a dose of antibiotics."

I could've sworn there was a hint of laughter in his eyes.

Chapter Twenty-Three

WALKER

"What the hell kind of fire are you playing with?" Jackson asked before taking a pull from his beer.

I twirled a bottle of beer between my fingers on the table. "What the hell are you talking about?" I countered.

Although I knew perfectly well what he was talking about. I was being stupid and reckless. I knew it, and I still couldn't stop it.

Jackson set his beer down and leaned back in his chair, hooking his elbow over the back of it. "Don't bullshit me, man. I don't know what's going on with you and Jade, but it's no fake thing. If you're not careful, Lucas is going to notice too."

I leaned my head back, letting out a sigh before leveling my gaze with his. "Right. I don't know what the fuck I'm doing. I guess I should talk to him."

"If you value your life, I would suggest you talk to Jade before you talk to her brother," Jackson said flatly. "Are you two a thing?"

"I don't know what we are, but it's not fake. I'm in over my head," I admitted, almost relieved to say it aloud.

Jackson chuckled. "Well, damn. I didn't expect Jade to ever fall for anyone, and I sure as hell didn't expect it to be you."

I masked the shock that sideswiped me at Jackson's teasing comment by taking a long swallow of my beer. Setting it down, I shrugged, hoping my tone sounded casual. "What do you mean?"

"I mean, I'm not blind. Nor is anyone else for that matter. I'm guessing Lucas either hasn't paid attention, or has decided not to say anything just yet. Don't underestimate him. He's a lot like you."

"Huh?" I asked brilliantly.

Jackson flashed a quick grin. "Kinda quiet, reserved. Makes it seem like he might not be a reactive kind of guy. When it comes to his family, he is."

I shook my head slowly, pressing my tongue inside my cheek. "Point taken. I'm not idiot enough to talk to him without letting Jade know first."

"Can't believe you're admitting there *is* something there."

I chuckled. "Only reason I'm admitting it is because I trust you to keep your fucking mouth shut."

"You can count on that. Well, except for Shay. I basically tell her everything. But she'll stay quiet. Plus, she already picked up on it, so it won't be coming from me," Jackson offered with a knowing grin.

"Oh hell," I muttered before draining my beer.

At that moment, Dawson came striding across the bar, hooking his hand on the back of a chair nearby and spinning it around as he sat down at our table. "Hey, y'all. Sorry I'm late. Evie made me drive."

"I take it that means you're not drinking," I teased as I watched Evie walking in with Shay, Dani, Valentina, and Jade.

"I'll pass. I could have one beer, but I'm just here to give y'all moral support."

"Are the other guys showing up?" I asked.

"What? You think I know everyone's schedule?" Dawson countered.

Jackson leveled his gaze on Dawson. "Yes. You always know everything, dude."

Dawson gave an easy shrug and a grin. "Boone and Grace are out, because I guess she wanted to watch a movie at home and their cat's not feeling well. Wade says he'll be on his way shortly. Dani said he went home to shower first. Lucas is home with his daughter since Valentina's out with the girls," Dawson explained, effectively demonstrating Jackson's point.

I didn't even want to contemplate the sense of relief that passed through me. I was being an idiot about Jade as it was, but Lucas's presence certainly complicated matters. I knew I needed to chat with him sooner rather than later.

Because, against all fucking odds, I was falling for Jade. I knew it, and I didn't even care. I only hoped I wasn't alone in it.

Every time I thought about Jade, emotion twined within my need for her like a vine, all the stronger as the fibers wound together. The word *love* feathered along the edges of my thoughts, and I shied away every time. Because I knew what it was to lose someone who mattered. I also knew what it was to let someone down.

I lost track of the conversation for a moment when I looked across the bar toward Jade. She was laughing at something. She had a glass of wine in her hand and was leaning her head back to take a sip. When it came to Jade, lust was my new master. My entire body vibrated with it from nothing more than a glance in her direction.

Dani reached for her drink from the bartender, and the group of women turned and began to approach our table. Jade's eyes caught mine from across the room. It felt as if that master cracked a whip, the snap of it sharp and electrifying. It sent a fiery sizzle through the air between us.

Evie had reached our table and was resting her hand on

Dawson's shoulder when Jackson murmured, so low I barely heard him, "Oh, fuck."

"What is it?" Shay asked when she stopped beside him, her brow furrowing in concern.

Jackson caught my eye before nudging his chin in a direction beyond my shoulder. Glancing over, I saw a man I'd never seen before walking out of the back hallway toward the bar.

Shay had followed Jackson's eyes as well. "Oh no." She looked at me. "You need to get Jade out of here."

Confused, I asked, "What are y'all talking about?"

Jade reached the table, hearing my question. "What's going on?" It didn't appear she'd heard Shay's comment.

My gut gave a decisive vibe when I saw the man who stopped by the bar. I didn't trust him. Not one bit. The hairs on the back of my neck rose. He was unremarkable—average height and average build with brown hair. He wore jeans and a T-shirt with a pair of tennis shoes.

Jade's face froze the moment she saw the man. I knew without being told that this had to be the guy who tried to spike her drink. Or rather, *had* spiked her drink but an observant waitress had prevented anything else from happening.

I was standing before I realized what I was doing. Meanwhile, Evie stepped away from Dawson's side and grabbed Jade's hand. "Don't even go over there. It is *not* worth it."

Jackson stood with me and spoke right at my shoulder. "Don't make a scene, man. Jade won't appreciate that."

"Doesn't pretty much everybody know what the hell went down? Why is he even here? I thought he got arrested," I muttered.

Shay had rounded the table to stand beside Jackson. Dani reached us and answered my question. "He was arrested, charged and so on. He served hardly any time. Because he didn't actually pull it off."

Unbelievably, the idiot looked over after he got a beer, his eyes locking on Jade. He began to approach our table. "Oh, hell no," Dani said, angling toward him.

My fists clenched, and I hadn't realized I started to move until Jackson gripped my arm, hard. I was strong, but so was Jackson.

"What the fuck, man?" I cast a frustrated glare over my shoulder before shaking my arm to free it.

"Dude, I get it. I'd like to clock him. I agree that he totally deserves it. Just don't do it in front of an audience. That's all I'm saying."

Jade strode directly to him with fire burning in her eyes. Dani was right beside her. "What the fuck are you doing here, Brad?"

Jade had plenty of loyal friends, and for that I was relieved. Jackson released my arm, and I walked over to stand beside Jade, not even thinking about it when I reached for her hand. Dani was on her other side, and the rest of our group clustered behind her.

Jade's hand was icy cold in mine, but she didn't swat me away. I could feel the tremor running through her, and fury burned through me in response. All I knew was a sketch of what had happened. But this man—Brad, apparently—had allegedly been Jade's friend, and he tried to drug her.

Jade narrowed her gaze on him as we all stood around her, her own personal backup team. "What the hell, Brad? Don't come anywhere near me."

Brad, asshole that he was, responded, "Jade, I'm not even on probation. I am allowed to be in public places. You never even gave me a chance to explain."

"There is no explanation that makes it okay for you to try to spike my drink with a date rape drug," Jade spat.

I sensed she was about to crack. Her eyes were bright with tears, and she was visibly shaking. Dani met my eyes, the concern evident in her gaze. Just then, one of the two bartenders approached. I didn't know Darren particularly well, but knew him to be a decent guy who didn't put up with much bullshit. He stopped beside Brad. "You need to leave," he said flatly.

"What the hell?" Brad protested. "I have a right to get a fucking drink."

Although I'd never laid eyes on Brad before, I sensed he wasn't accustomed to much confrontation. I imagined what little time he spent behind bars hadn't been particularly pleasant for him.

Darren shrugged. "This is a private business. You may have a right to get a drink, generally speaking, but we don't have to serve you. If we ask you to leave, you have to leave. Now, we can do this one way, or another. You can walk out and leave the bottle on the counter. I didn't see you come in, and our new bartender doesn't know who you are. If he did, you wouldn't have been served. You can walk out on your own, or I'll escort you. Take your pick."

Brad glanced around and muttered something under his breath. "Fuck y'all," he added, raising his voice before turning and stalking away. He tossed his almost full beer in the trashcan by the door to the back hallway, just hard enough against the wall that it broke before it fell in the trashcan.

I heard Darren speaking to Jade. "Sorry about that, Jade. I didn't see him come in."

Shay was saying something to her as well.

Confident no one was going to leave Jade alone, I leaned over, giving Jade's hand a squeeze. "I'll be right back."

Releasing her hand, I followed Brad out, barely hearing Jackson behind me. "What the hell are you doing, man?" he asked as he jogged to catch up to me when I was about halfway down the back hallway.

"Don't worry, I won't get myself arrested. You're welcome to tag along."

Jackson muttered something under his breath, but he stayed with me.

I slammed through the back door out to the parking lot, my eyes landing on Brad as he walked. I closed the distance between us quickly. The moment I caught up to him, I grabbed his arm and spun him around.

"What the—" he began.

"Here's the deal. Stay the hell away from Jade." I stepped right up to him, almost chest to chest.

"Who the hell are you?"

"A friend. Unlike you."

Jackson hung back, but he was right there, and I knew he would step in if needed. Considering we didn't have an audience, I didn't think he was going to do a damned thing unless things got out of hand.

Brad, apparently on the slow side, laughed. "Right. I've known Jade a hell of a lot longer than you. It was all a big misunderstanding."

Before I could form a thought, I had curled my fist into his shirt and lifted him, stepping to press him against a truck just to the side of us. "Bullshit. Everyone knows what happened. You got caught slipping a drug in Jade's drink. There were witnesses. Only assholes and cowards pull shit like that. Obviously you couldn't get what you wanted when Jade was conscious, so you had to try to pull that. You can tell yourself all day it was a big misunderstanding. It wasn't. If you don't leave her alone, I'll make sure you regret it." I shoved him back with a disgusted growl. "Now, get the fuck out of here."

Brad looked from me to Jackson, protesting, "Aren't you a first responder? Did you see what he just did?"

Jackson laughed. "Good luck with that. You don't have any friends in this town. You can either keep playing stupid, or get the hell out of here."

Brad stared at us for a beat before spinning and jogging across the parking lot to climb into his car. Jackson and I waited in silence until the sound of the gravel crunching under his wheels ended as he turned out of the parking lot onto the road.

When I glanced back toward the bar, I saw Jade standing in the doorway with Shay beside her.

Chapter Twenty-Four

JADE

My heart was thumping hard against my ribs, and I had a sick, twisty feeling in my gut. I stared at Walker across the parking lot.

"Are you okay?" Shay asked from my side.

I didn't break my gaze from Walker's. Although I couldn't sort out a single feeling, looking into his eyes, even from a distance, helped me to settle inside. Something clicked into place inside, and I finally managed a deep breath before I turned to look at Shay.

"I'm pissed off, but I'm okay."

"Pissed off..." Her words petered out when she looked toward Walker and Jackson, who were approaching us now.

By this point, Walker and Jackson reached us. Walker was fairly vibrating with energy. He had it in check—because he was always self-contained—but I could sense the tension humming through him. I wasn't going to lie; it'd been just a little bit—okay maybe *a lot*—satisfying to see him so easily lift Brad and give him a shake.

Brad was such a coward. That's what I told him that night. Trying to drug me to likely rape me was more cowardly than just raping me. I realized how insane that sounded. My therapist had told me it was perfectly fine to think thoughts like that. She said it was part of my process.

Before I thought about it, I was stepping close to Walker and reaching for his hand. His eyes were searching my face. The sound of Jackson clearing his throat snapped into the moment of silence as Walker and I stared at each other.

Whipping my head in Jackson's direction, I considered him for a moment. I flicked my eyes from Walker to Jackson and back. "Thank you, both. I still can't believe Brad just showed up here. I've covered shifts here for years. Brad had to know there was a chance he'd see me if he came here."

"He's an asshole," Shay said forcefully. "We all used to be friendly with him." She looked toward Walker. I supposed she was trying to explain.

Walker inclined his head. His hand was firm around mine, and his thumb brushed back and forth on the sensitive skin on the inside of my wrist.

Fire feathered outward from there, moving over my skin like a breath of air. I couldn't explain any of what I was feeling. Brad's presence had unsettled me. When Shay and I followed Walker and Jackson down the hallway, I'd felt cranky and irritated. I didn't need Walker to protect me, yet he had.

He was so alpha, so instinctively protective. I couldn't believe how it made me feel. Although part of me wanted to push against it, I also savored it and wanted to envelope myself in his strength.

"You ready to go?" Walker asked, his tone low.

I nodded because I couldn't find any more words. He was turning away with my hand in his before I realized we hadn't said anything to Shay and Jackson. Glancing back, I saw the understanding in her expression.

Shay's eyes searched my face before she said, "Good night."

Walker looked at Jackson. "Thanks, man."

Jackson shrugged. "I'll be your backup anytime. 'Specially when it's not in the middle of a crowd."

Walker chuckled, and we kept walking until we reached his truck. "How'd you get here?"

"I hitched a ride with Shay. Are you giving me a ride home?"

"Absolutely," he replied, his voice raspy, right before bending low and fitting his mouth over mine.

Whether Walker knew how much I wanted him didn't really matter. All that mattered was his lips on mine, and the feel of his strong arms pulling me close.

He turned us, pressing my back against his truck. The feel of the cool steel sifted through my thin cotton blouse, a marked contrast to the fire burning me up inside. By the time he gentled our kiss, leaning his forehead against mine as we both gulped in heaving breaths of air, I'd completely forgotten we were in a parking lot. A very public parking lot, as evidenced by the sound of a car door slamming and voices drifting over to us.

"We should go," he murmured.

His lips were still so close to mine I could feel the subtle motion of them. Each brushing touch kindled the fire hotter and hotter inside of me. When I opened my eyes and collided with his, I was jolted by the sense of intimacy enveloping us. For several beats of my heart, his thumping in time with mine because I could feel it pressed against my chest, panic clawed at me inside.

Not fear related to Walker in the sense that he might do anything to hurt me. I had absolute faith that he wouldn't. That very faith was what sent the wheels of panic spinning madly, scrambling to catch purchase and keep me from falling deeper and deeper into the abyss.

The idea that my trust was faulty terrified me. Because I'd been so thoroughly proven wrong before.

Just as the claws of panic sank deeply, Walker straightened slightly, lifting a hand to brush my hair back. His hand slid down to cup my cheek with his thumb resting over my bottom lip. "Let's go."

I didn't know what it was about his touch, but that alone was enough to quell the panic, to soothe the ragged edges of my oh-so-untrusting heart. I was falling in love with Walker, and I didn't know what the hell to do about it. Because it was the only thing that seemed to make sense, I nodded wordlessly. I let myself stay caught in the super-powered beam of his gaze just long enough to ignore the distant voice clamoring inside that I needed to be careful, that I needed not to dare to put myself at risk again.

You see, the temptation to have another night with Walker was far more powerful than anything else. Reason and logic didn't stand a chance. They were as weak as a piece of tissue caught in the wind of a storm.

———

By the time Walker rolled his truck to a stop in front of his house, my entire body felt like molten liquid. It had been— at best—a ten-minute drive. The entire time, he kept one sexy hand on the steering wheel and the other resting above my knee. His thumb occasionally brushed over my skin, just below the hem of my skirt.

Licks of fire radiated from that spot, feathering through my entire body until I was thrumming and nearly frantic with need. He'd asked me whether I wanted to go to his place or mine. Out of curiosity, I said his. Because I hadn't been inside his place yet even though it was just down the street from mine.

I was only regretting that curiosity because I was so impatient. As soon as he cut the engine, he was out of his truck in a flash and opening the passenger side door for me. Because he just had to go and be handsome, sexy, a bit mysterious, and a freaking gentleman on top of it all. If I ever took him home to meet my parents, my mother would swoon.

As soon as the door shut behind me, I didn't quite know how to read the expression crossing his face. He shook his head, almost as if to himself, and mouthed, "No."

Then, his hand was curling around mine as we began walking swiftly across the gravel driveway. We stopped in front of the door to the side of the house with a light shining above the entrance under the arched roof overhead.

"No, what?" I asked as he turned the key in the lock and pushed the door open.

Walker didn't reply at first, tossing his keys on the table by the door as he closed the door behind us. Just as I was about to repeat my question, he spun me around. My back collided with the door, not too hard, but hard enough that I gasped.

He stilled instantly as he stood several electric inches away from me. "Are you okay?" His tone was low and intent. I sensed a leashed energy to him.

"Uh-huh. You just caught me off guard."

Our eyes locked. The air felt charged, as if it had captured a bolt of lightning and the power was vibrating around us with electric sparks striking from the force of attraction between us. I took an unsteady breath.

Walker snapped his eyes from mine as he leaned his head back, his shoulders rising as he gulped in a breath. When he leveled his gaze with mine again, the look there snatched my breath away and sent a blast of heat through my body. "I don't think I can be a gentleman," he bit out.

Although his words were polite, his voice was ragged and taut.

"Just fuck me."

Walker's lips kicked up at one corner as he laughed softly, the sound almost tortured. "Damn, girl, you know exactly what I want."

I happened to be wearing a skirt. It wasn't anything particularly sexy, but it was sure comfortable, and I could pull off a night out with the girls with cowboy boots and look halfway decent. Walker made quick work of getting it out of the way and dragged it up around my hips. I reached between us, palming his cock through his jeans before swiftly tearing open the buttons on his fly. I let out a satisfied sigh when I shoved his boxers down and his cock sprang free.

I hadn't even noticed Walker was already pushing my panties out of the way. With my cowboy boots still on, he lifted me—so easily—in his arms, and pressed my back against the door. In another fiery second, I felt the thick crown of his cock press against my entrance.

I wasn't thinking. Not at all. I was caught in the rushing current of need driving me forward. When Walker growled "Oh fuck," I barely registered it. Curling my legs around his hips, I arched into him, feeling my slick juices slide over his length.

"I need a—" he began.

I had no patience. "I'm on the pill. Just fuck me."

Walker—because he was that gentleman I mentioned earlier—held still. I opened my eyes to find his searching my face. "Are you sure?"

"Yes! I need you inside me now."

Thank God he could follow orders.

His forehead fell to mine as he held still for a beat before surging swiftly inside me, filling me completely in one deep stroke.

"Oh God," I murmured. My words were slurred. It felt so good to have him filling and stretching me. The sensation was intense.

Chapter Twenty-Five

WALKER

My heartbeat thundered as I savored the feel of Jade's slick core sheathing me. She felt so good. So right. There was sex, and then there was whatever this was with Jade. It was beyond anything within my prior experience.

Raw, primitive need had overtaken me, and I couldn't wait. This was no skilled seduction. I simply needed her. I needed this. With my lips a whisper away from hers, I murmured, "Hold on, sweetheart."

Then, I fucked her hard and fast against the door. She was with me for every stroke. Her skirt was bunched around her hips and my jeans were just barely out of the way.

My release was building rapidly, crashing like a dam about to burst as the pressure built and built. Adjusting her weight in my arms, I was relieved for the door behind us to give me an assist. I reached between us with my free hand, finding her swollen clit instantly. With a little tease, her pussy clamped down over my cock, and she cried out my name in a husky shout with her head falling against the door.

The pressure inside me finally let loose, my release slamming through me so hard as it poured into her. By the time it was over, my forehead had fallen into the dip of her shoulder as I struggled for breath. I savored every little tremor in her body.

As consciousness filtered in, I became aware that my fingers were digging into the sweet curve of her bottom on one side. I released my grip slowly and lifted my head. When I opened my eyes and saw her, I almost became hard again. Which was downright incredible considering I'd just come harder than I ever had in my life.

Jade, with her dark hair a tangled mess around her shoulders, her shirt twisted sideways, and her skin flushed with her lips pink and swollen from our kisses was simply a sight to behold. She was so sexy and sultry, she simply took my breath away. Her thick dark lashes swept up, and she met my gaze.

"Didn't mean to be so rough," I said.

She shook her head. "Please don't apologize."

I stared at her, my heart still thundering. Unable to form any sensible response, I leaned forward and brushed my lips over hers briefly before pulling back with an effort. I wanted to stay buried deep inside of her.

Don't get me wrong, a small part of that urge was born solely out of how deeply my need for her ran. Jade had tapped into a vein so deep inside of me I hadn't even known it was there. The madness she wrought—a tangle of lust, pure need, and an emotional connection so visceral it frightened me—left me almost shaky inside. Being intimately connected with her anchored and eased me.

Because I needed to trick myself into thinking I was in control, I snatched what little I had and withdrew from her. I stepped back and slowly lowered her to the floor.

I wasn't afraid of my feelings. On the contrary, I was almost relieved. Because I could be accused of being cynical, I'd been afraid that perhaps I *was* too cynical to fall for anyone like this.

As I tucked myself in and buttoned my jeans, I watched

her putting her clothes to rights and smoothing her skirt into place. It felt as if she had reached right in my chest and snatched my heart because she most surely held it in her hands.

What I feared was the way her eyes shuttered slightly as we looked at each other. I knew without even a little doubt that Jade was seriously guarded. I knew trust wasn't something she handed out casually. As Jackson had presciently noted, I was going to have to work for her.

"Did you even have dinner tonight?" I asked.

Jade stared at me for a moment before shaking her head. "No. I meant to grab something at the bar, but obviously that didn't happen."

"I'll make us something."

"You cook?" she asked, her brows hitching in surprise.

I nodded with a soft laugh. "I do. I'm told I'm good at it. Let's see what I've got to work with."

As I turned away to walk into my kitchen, I considered that perhaps I needed to make a habit of surprising Jade. That seemed to knock her guard down slightly.

Chapter Twenty-Six

JADE

"JJ, look!" Rylie called to me from the kitchen table where she was working on a drawing.

I finished loading the dishwasher and closed it before I turned. Crossing the kitchen, I slipped into the chair beside her. "Let me see."

My niece turned the small whiteboard in her hands and held it up. An explosion of color covered the entire board. Angling my head to the side, I studied it. "Is that a pig I see there?" I smiled.

"Yes!" Rylie exclaimed, giving me a toothy grin. As soon as she set the whiteboard down, she promptly erased everything she'd done. I'd gotten her this whiteboard about a month ago, and it could keep her occupied for hours at a time.

"How loose is that tooth?" I asked when she distractedly wiggled a loose front tooth with her fingers.

"I don't know," she said. "It keeps wiggling. The last one hurt when it came out."

My little niece looked so much like my brother it made my heart hurt sometimes. With her glossy dark hair that had a curl to it and her big green eyes, she was definitely a Cole family member. The only thing I could see of her mother in her features was her round button nose. I considered her blessed for that. Although a strong, bold nose looked good on Lucas, on me, I considered it too big.

I doubted Rylie would ever remember her mother. Melissa had an aneurysm when Rylie wasn't even one year old, and it was over before she made it to the hospital.

Rylie brought my attention back to her. "Should we pull it out?"

"Nah. Let's wait and let your dad figure out when it's time for that tooth to come out."

Rylie bent her head down, biting her lower lip as her brow furrowed once she began to focus on her next work of art. "Valentine promised she would decide this time." Rylie had always called Valentina Valentine. With Valentina and Lucas going strong, I hoped they would make it official soon. No matter what Rylie called her, Valentina was becoming her mother in every way that counted as far as taking care of her.

"Oh, so your dad's not in charge of that anymore?"

"Last time, Daddy said a tooth was ready to come out, and it wasn't."

"Always smart to listen to Valentina," I replied with a solemn nod.

As if conjured by our discussion of her wisdom, the front door opened, and Valentina came in, her arms laden with grocery bags.

I jumped up from the table, hurrying over. "Do you need some help?"

Valentina's red curls bounced when she shook her head. "There's nothing left to get. I always carry more than I should."

I helped unload from her arms, and we began putting the groceries away. Until Valentina had moved in, I'd spent three or four days a week at Lucas's house because I was his main daycare person when Rylie wasn't in school. She was only now finishing first grade. He paid me quite well, but having Valentina in their lives meant he didn't need my help nearly as much.

Not that I'd ever minded taking care of Rylie, not even a little, but I was beyond pleased Valentina was here for Lucas and Rylie. It gave me the opportunity to get my focus back on track for my life. Sometimes that felt good, but I still felt like I was middling along.

I watched as Valentina leaned over and dropped a kiss on Rylie's dark hair. The easy relationship they had warmed my heart. A small part of me suddenly wondered if I might ever have anything like that.

I'd comfortably lived with the idea that I didn't even want anything like that. And then, Walker came along.

"How was today?" Valentina asked as she straightened.

I put a can of olives on the shelf in one of the cabinets, replying, "Just great. I wasn't sure when you'd be back."

Valentina shrugged. "Me neither. It took longer than I planned. I went with Lucas for his physical in Asheville, and then we did some errands. I dropped him off at the lodge and came home. I didn't know if you were working tonight at the bar," she said, glancing my way as she closed the refrigerator after putting away a few items.

"Not tonight."

"Are you planning on looking for anything else for work? Dani is always scouting out wait staff for the lodge."

I smiled. "Not that I would mind working there, but I make more money as a bartender. If she wanted me to cover some bartending shifts, I'd be all over that."

"I'll let her know. Another guy quit recently because he moved out of town with his girlfriend."

"I'd be happy to fill in there." I leaned my hips against the counter as I reached for the cup of coffee I'd left there earlier and took a sip. "I need to figure out what the hell I wanna do."

I quickly slapped my hand over my mouth, realizing I'd said "hell." I was usually pretty well trained around Riley, but every now and then I spaced it.

So absorbed in whatever she was drawing, Rylie didn't even notice. Valentina flashed me a quick grin.

I took another sip and lowered my cup. "This is luke-warm, and I could use some fresh coffee. Should I make a pot?"

Valentina nodded. "That would be excellent. I didn't get enough coffee this morning, and I've got some bookkeeping to catch up on tonight for the lodge."

While I got the coffee started, Valentina paused beside Rylie, her hand on her shoulder. "I had a phone call on my way home. You know the new girl who lives across the street?" At Rylie's nod, Valentina continued, "Her mom invited you over to help bake cookies. Do you want to go over there?"

I tapped the start button just in time to see Rylie's head bouncing with her enthusiastic nod. "When can I go?" She scrambled out of her chair.

"As soon as you clean up the table here. Unless there's more mess that I need to check with Jade about." Valentina glanced at me.

"Not a thing. She's all set. I heard about this new friend. Remind me of her name again," I said.

"Torie." Rylie dutifully picked up the eraser and wiped off what she'd been drawing. Needing no further instruction, she put all her markers and the whiteboard away in the little cubby she had on a bench by the kitchen door. "I'm ready," she announced.

"Be right back. I'm just gonna walk across the street with her."

With Rylie skipping at Valentina's side, I watched as they departed. Moments later, Valentina returned, sitting down at the kitchen table with a sigh. "Today ended up being a long day."

"Yeah?" I asked as I filled two mugs with coffee and carried them to the table. After fetching the cream from the refrigerator, I sat down across from her.

"Yeah, there was nothing in particular. It was just everything took longer than I expected. We had to wait for almost an hour for Lucas to get in for his physical and then ran around doing errands. Now, I'm going to bury my head in numbers for a few hours. I don't mind telling you, it's really awesome that Rylie has a friend across the street now. I actually like the mom, and we can give each other breaks."

I smiled. "I bet. Plus, major bonus is Rylie has another friend. I swear, that little girl is so social. She's nothing like Lucas."

Valentina grinned. "He is much quieter than her."

I threw my head back with a laugh at her dry tone. "I'd say. It's hard not to be quieter than Rylie."

Valentina laughed softly before asking, "What was her mother like? Lucas almost never talks about her."

I thought about Melissa. "Melissa was average social. Rylie's something else. I mean, according to her teacher last year, she was the most social kid in her class."

"I know. The only thing she ever gets in trouble for in school is talking to her friends in class. Fortunately, she handles redirection well."

I laughed. "She certainly didn't get her social butterfly gene from me."

"You and Lucas are a lot alike. Always keeping to yourself and holding back a little. You're a little more friendly than him even though you did scare me to death when I first knew him."

I grinned. "I'm a protective sister because he got burned. Maybe I was a bit much. Once I realized how awesome you were, I was totally on team Valentina."

She flashed a grateful smile. "Thank you for that. Speaking of things like dating, what *is* going on with you and Walker?"

I masked my initial reaction with a sip of coffee, although I could feel my cheeks heating and hoped it wasn't enough for Valentina to notice. When I looked back over at her, I saw nothing but warmth and understanding in her gaze. Maybe, just maybe, a hint of teasing.

After another sip of my coffee, I decided to be honest. "I don't know. It all started because of that fake wedding date." I sighed and traced my fingertip in a circle around the base of my coffee mug.

"Maybe that date wasn't so fake after all."

Chapter Twenty-Seven

JADE

"It was supposed to be. It's just... Well, in case you didn't notice, Walker's totally hot."

Valentina nodded firmly. "For sure. He's not my type, but it'd be hard not to notice. Although I don't feel that way about him, he's got a little bit of that same tall, dark, and mysterious vibe Lucas had."

"Had?" I teased.

Valentina's cheeks went pink. "Well, it's not so mysterious anymore. He's still tall, dark, and sexy."

"Enough about how amazing my brother is," I teased.

Valentina sipped her coffee and tilted her head to the side. "Fine with me. Tell me what's going on with you and Walker?"

"I don't know. I didn't plan on this." I seemed to have an abundance of saying and thinking that when it came to contemplating whatever was happening between Walker and me.

"I know *that*. You made it perfectly clear that you intended to never date again. I have to admit, I was a little puzzled about that."

"Getting serious means trusting someone enough to know that they're not full of shit. I don't even have to tell you how hard that is. Just look at my life. I thought Brad was my friend. People lie and bullshit all the time to people they allegedly care about. Not to speak ill of the dead, but look at what Melissa did to Lucas. The reason I offered to be Walker's date was because he didn't want his ex-girlfriend pestering him to try to get back together after she screwed around behind his back with his best friend's brother. That guy's an asshole who apparently has screwed around on her plenty. Although, I hear she's done the same. They deserve each other. That's just a few examples close to me. Should I continue?"

Valentina leveled me with a pointed look. "Do you think Lucas would lie to me? I'm not talking about screwing around on me, more generally speaking."

"Oh my God! No. He would never do that."

"How about Jackson to Shay?"

Now, I sent a pointed glare in her direction. "I see where you're going with this. Obviously Jackson would never lie to Shay."

Anxiety began to twist in my chest. I hated that feeling. In fact, it was this jumble of feelings I had sworn to avoid forever—uncertainty, worry that I might trust the wrong person, worry that someone would do something I didn't expect, something horribly wrong.

After a fortifying sip of my coffee, I drummed my fingertips on the table. "It's not that simple. I don't know how much Lucas has told you—"

Valentina interjected. "Most of it. I can understand why you worry you might trust the wrong person. That's a risk we all have to take. Do you trust Walker?"

Valentina, being Valentina, never hesitated to strip away the veneer in a conversation and go straight to the painful core of an issue.

"Yes," I said, rather reluctantly. I wanted to say the opposite, but that wasn't fair to Walker.

After a moment, she nodded slowly. "I see. It's easier if you don't, isn't it?"

"Yes! Exactly."

"Not to get too personal, but I always wondered when you said you never planned to date if you meant that you never intended to have sex again."

I shrugged. "That was the plan. Let's face it, not all sex is good. In fact, statistically speaking, most women don't have great experiences."

Valentina opened her mouth to say something, but I held my hand up. "Oh, for God's sake. Do *not* talk to me about your sex life with my brother. I'm not a prude, but please don't. Just don't."

Valentina shrugged. "Fine. It just seems kind of extreme to plan to never date or have sex at your age."

"You know, there are some incredible sex toys. You should know, that's what brought you and Lucas together to begin with," I teased.

Valentina burst out laughing, her cheeks tingeing pink as she nodded.

Although my brother had never discussed it with me, it was a running joke among those of us who were friends with her. She'd ordered a vibrator in the mail, and it accidentally got delivered to Lucas. That mishap set the wheels in motion for them to fall in love.

"I'm not asking about Walker specifically, but is a vibrator really better?" she asked when she stopped laughing.

My cheeks got a little hot again. The moment she asked that, my mind flashed to the night before when I was so frantic for him, and he had me against the door half-dressed. That, along with every other encounter with him, ranked as the best sex I'd ever had. Much as I was loath to admit it, even my favorite vibrator paled in comparison.

"You made your point," I mumbled.

Conveniently, as far as I was concerned, Valentina's cell phone rang. Glancing down at the screen on her phone, she said, "I need to get this. It's Shay."

She took the call, while I stood to refill my coffee. She held her mug up when I turned back, so I did the same for her. While she chatted with Shay about something to do with the accounts at the lodge, I wiped down the counter and checked the calendar on my phone for my schedule at the bar.

Before I began babysitting full-time for Lucas, I still hadn't formed a clear plan for my life. I'd been working as a bartender and trying, to no avail, to figure out when I could start my pie in the sky landscaping business. That meant money, and I still didn't have tons of that.

For now, my bar shifts covered the basics, and I was slowly paying off my student loans. I felt at loose ends, and it seemed safer and easier just to coast along the way I was. Making a major decision about work felt like too much. Although I didn't like to think about it often, much of my life had faded into indecision after what happened with Brad. It was like I couldn't trust myself to make a single decision. Because I had *never* seen that coming.

The front door opened and Lucas came striding through. "Hey, sis," he called as he dropped his bag by the door before crossing the room to lean against the counter that served as a divider between the kitchen and the open style living room.

"Hey. Coffee?"

"Always."

Fetching another mug out of the cabinet, I quickly filled it and handed it over. After a sip, Lucas eyed me for a minute. Because I knew my brother well, I knew he was about to jump into a topic I might not appreciate.

"What?"

He gave me a long look. "What's that tone for?"

"You've got the look that says you're about to bring up something I won't like."

"That's a specific look?"

"Yes. I've known you my whole life. It's a very specific look. Cut to the chase."

"I heard Brad showed up at the bar last night. Just wondering if you're okay."

"I'm fine."

"I'm planning to go talk to him."

I groaned. "I do *not* need you to go talk to him. I handled it." I hated feeling like people thought they needed to look out for me. It scratched with sharp claws at all of my defenses. I didn't need anyone.

"I know you did. I also know you got an assist from Walker and Jackson. According to Jackson, Walker almost started a fight with Brad."

"So what if he did?" I countered, my tone mulish.

"Okay, I'll talk to you later," I heard Valentina saying to Shay.

"I'd like to hit Brad myself. I'll have to thank Walker for having your back. Is something going on with him?"

"Oh my God," I muttered, setting my coffee cup down. "It's none of your business."

Lucas's gaze only grew more concerned. I knew I was overreacting, but ugh. I was beyond unsettled. All of this with Walker, Brad showing up and reminding me how much I couldn't trust myself, and just how twisted up inside I felt. Now, to have my older brother coming in and pressing every single one of my giant buttons, well, it sent anger spinning into the storm of muddled emotions already brewing inside.

"I gotta go." I spun around and snatched my purse off the chair where I'd left it earlier.

Valentina stood from the table, her eyes worried. When I looked toward Lucas, it was clear he realized he had overstepped. "Jade—" he began.

I shook my head sharply. "I know. You're sorry. I need to go because I have a shift. Call me if you need me to babysit."

With tears in my eyes and my throat aching and tight, I had to get the hell out of there and fast. Hurrying past both of them, I bolted out the front door.

Chapter Twenty-Eight

WALKER

I took off my leather gloves and tossed them on the table beside me. Reaching over, I turned off the miter saw and grabbed the water bottle sitting in the open windowsill. After drinking almost half of it, I leaned my hips against the table as I looked around the space.

Last summer before I started here, Jackson had begun adding new studio guest cabins. With Stolen Hearts Lodge flourishing and becoming busier, they needed more space. These high-end private little cabins were like catnip for the guests who wanted some sort of outdoorsy experience without actually being required to camp.

They had every bell and whistle you could imagine and were gorgeous. I'd mostly taken over handling the hardwood flooring with a little help from Lucas and Jackson. Among many things my father had done, he'd been a high-end carpenter. I knew how to lay a gorgeous hardwood floor, including creating patterns and making it almost a work of art.

I'd spent the morning designing the layout and cutting the flooring for this studio. We'd settled on a starburst pattern centered in front of the river stone fireplace that would eventually be built. For the most part, I spent most of these jobs on my own until it came time to lay the flooring. Then, I had the help of any of the guys because installing the flooring was much faster with a team.

"How's it going in here?" a voice carried in through the open doorway.

The days were getting hot, so I preferred to get most of this done in the morning. I could handle the heavy labor with sweat dripping, but the detail work was more annoying when it was boiling hot outside.

Lucas stepped in, his gaze bouncing from me to scan around the room and settle on the neatly stacked pile of flooring ready to be installed.

"We're ready to roll. I'm gonna head up to the lodge to grab a bite. Are you available to help me this afternoon?"

Lucas nodded, holding my gaze just long enough that a prickle of unease ran down my spine. Obviously, I hadn't forgotten that Jade was Lucas's younger sister. Yet, I'd basically shut that detail out of my mind whenever I happened to be around him. I liked and respected Lucas and guessed he might be pissed if he knew what was going on between Jade and me.

Whether or not he knew I was thinking about Jade, he commented, "I meant to thank you."

"For what?" I lifted the water bottle again and took another few swallows.

"Getting that asshole away from Jade a few nights ago. Jackson mentioned what happened."

"Of course. I'd do the same for anyone."

On its face, that comment was entirely truthful. That said, it wasn't likely that I would be as fired up as I'd been. Jade had come to mean far more to me than I'd been prepared to handle.

Lucas nodded. "I know you would." He slid a hand in the pocket of his jeans, leaning out the other open windowsill and looking through the trees. The day was beginning to heat up, the air heavy with humidity. A drop of sweat rolled down my spine.

Lucas looked back at me, his gaze assessing. "What's going on with you and my sister?"

It didn't slip my notice that he called her "my sister" rather than simply saying her name.

Oh fuck. This was the part where I should have spoken to Jade about this possibility. Lucas was no idiot.

I didn't look away as these thoughts spun through my mind. I finally settled on the only answer I could live with because I didn't want to out and out lie to Lucas. "Can I take a rain check on answering?"

I knew my answer would be revealing, but it gave me the chance I needed to talk to Jade first. That was its own quagmire. I'd gone and fallen in love with her.

Holding Jade's heart was like holding spun sugar in my hands. As feisty and guarded as she could be, I knew what lay under the surface was fragile. She'd let her doubts rule her. She was a vulnerable woman who was strong and loyal and so damn sexy I didn't think she'd ever stop taking my breath away.

Lucas's eyes fairly bored through me. After a very long moment, during which my heart beat out the drum line to an anxious tune, he nodded slowly. "You can."

He went quiet, and I could see the muscle in his jaw clenching as he turned to look out the window again. I held my silence, waiting for whatever he had to say next. Because I knew he had more to say.

Turning back, he leveled me with another hard look. "Do not fucking hurt my sister."

Lucas, never one to be particularly chatty—a quality I appreciated because I shared it—walked out after that. He called over his shoulder a second later, "Catch you at lunch. We can knock this floor out this afternoon."

———

Later that evening, I parked my truck in front of Jade's house. I'd seen her briefly when I stopped by to check on Everett before I left for work. She was checking on him on her way back from a lunch shift at the bar.

Although we hadn't had much of a chance to talk, she'd nodded when I asked her if it was okay to stop by tonight. As I sat in my truck with the quiet settling around me, I became uncomfortably aware of the steady beat of my heart and anxiety twisting in my gut. I didn't consider myself an anxious man.

In fact, my nerves were usually so steady that the sensation inside was completely unfamiliar to me. Here I thought I'd never fall for anyone, and I'd tripped and stumbled right into love with Jade. I was pretty sure she didn't want to be in love.

The only thing that was certain was that I had to talk to her. Before Lucas said something. I'd never been one to delay, so I figured I would barrel through this just like I did anything else. I wasn't a first responder for nothing. I was solid in a crisis. I hoped those nerves would help me through this.

I stepped out of my truck and closed the door, pausing for a moment to look ahead. Although I'd been offered the option to live in one of those cute studio cabins I was building at the lodge, I passed it over. I liked my privacy, and I'd lucked into a house my grandmother left to me. Like my place, Jade's house offered a clear view of Stolen Hearts Valley. The mountain ridge on the far side of the valley was a dark silhouette with the moon rising behind it. The sound of crickets chirping filled the air.

I took a breath and walked to the door. Whether I liked it or not, Lucas asking me about Jade forced my hand. A moment passed after I knocked before she opened the door. She'd changed out of her jeans and T-shirt into a pair of fitted shorts and a black V-neck T-shirt. The sight of Jade with her hair pulled up in a ponytail and her skin fresh and rosy as if she'd just showered slammed into me. She seemed almost sweet. Jade *was* sweet and I knew it, but I knew she'd argue that point.

"Hey," she said, holding the door open and gesturing me through.

I stepped past her, stuffing my hands in my pockets, solely for the purpose of containing the urge to grab her and kiss her senseless.

Whether she sensed the tension coiled tightly inside of me, she didn't let it show. She walked past me. "I'm having a glass of wine. Do you want something to drink?"

I followed her through the living room and into her kitchen.

"I'm not much of a wine guy," I replied, sitting down on the stool she pointed toward as she walked to the counter to pick up her glass of wine and take a sip.

Lowering it, her lips quirked in a smile. "Walker, I'm a bartender. I have more than wine. I've got vodka and scotch. I'm all out of beer, though."

"I'll take a scotch if you have it."

"It's the good kind," she said with the sly smile. "On the rocks?" She pulled out a clear glass tumbler and a bottle from a cabinet.

"Nope. Just plain scotch."

In another moment, she slid the glass across the counter to me. Lifting it, I took a swallow. The rich, nutty flavor slid across my tongue, smooth and satisfying. "Damn, that's good."

Jade grinned and sat down across from me. We were seated only a few feet apart, and somehow the distance felt like too much. I took another healthy swallow of my drink. Although a sense of calm was buoying me, I was about to try to talk about my feelings. Something I had very little experience with and never expected to worry about.

Jade saved me by commenting, "So, Jackson says Everett probably won't be able to be released back into the wild." Her mouth twisted as disappointment flashed across her face.

"Oh? I didn't have a chance to talk to him about it today. That's too bad. What happens when that's the case?"

"I was about to ask Jackson the same thing when his next appointment showed up. I'm assuming he just stays at the rescue."

I nodded, taking another sip of my scotch. "We'll find out."

Jade took a swallow of her wine, and I watched as she leaned her head back slightly. Only Jade had this effect on me. Every small thing she did set a low hum of electricity vibrating through my body, tapping into this bone-deep need for her. I decided I needed to just get this over with.

"Lucas asked me today what was going on with us."

Jade narrowed her eyes, her lips tightening in a line before she spoke. "Are you serious?"

"Why would I make that up?"

She took a gulp of her wine. She sighed as she lowered the glass. "I love my brother, but sometimes he's overprotective."

I shrugged. "He's your brother. Can't say I blame him. If I had a sister, I'd probably be the same way."

"Probably?" A smile teased at the corners of her mouth.

I felt a grin tugging at mine as I nodded. "Okay, definitely."

"What did you tell him?"

"I figured I was in a no-win situation. No matter what I did or didn't say, unless I lied, I was in a bind."

"And, you're not a liar."

She was right, but I didn't know what to think of how good it made me feel that she had faith I would be honest.

"I asked him for a rain check."

Jade found that hysterical, her shoulders shaking with

laughter. "Seriously?" she asked when she finally finished laughing. "How did Lucas handle that?"

"He accepted my answer, but told me I'd better not hurt you. I didn't wanna say anything else until you and I talked."

"I do appreciate that."

"I guess you might need to be ready for him to ask you about it."

"Oh, I'm sure he will. I suppose we should talk." Jade looked uncertain. Her eyes bounced from me down to her wine glass. She traced along the edge of the counter with her fingertip.

After another sip of scotch, I laid it out there. "I didn't expect this. Not at all. Oh, I knew I was attracted to you, but I thought I could keep it in hand. Even after the wedding, I thought things would fade. Can I be really blunt with you?"

Jade lifted her head, her eyes catching mine. She looked surprised. After a nod, she waited quietly while my heart kicked against my ribs.

"I think I'm falling in love with you. I know you planned never to date anyone, so I'm not sure how you feel about that," I finally said.

As nervous as I was, the words came out normal. A strange sense of relief washed through me. Saying aloud how I felt was a relief if only because it was honest.

Jade's eyes widened slightly. I could see the rapid flutter of her pulse along the side of her neck. Her cheeks flushed, and she took a quick breath as she stared at me.

"If you're worried about it, I don't expect you to say the same in return," I added. Although it stung a bit to say that, I meant it.

"I don't know what to say," Jade finally said.

"I figured I might as well tell you. This is real for me. Lucas is only going to accept my rain check for so long. Either I lie to him, or I tell him the truth. I prefer to be honest."

Jade lifted her wine glass and took a swallow. Her hand shook slightly when she set the glass down. I instinctively reached over, curling my hand over hers.

"Are you okay? I don't know how to move forward. Maybe this means that you tell me to fuck off. I won't lie and pretend that's what I want, but—"

Jade shook her head sharply. When she didn't say anything, I said, "I'm not sure what that means."

"I didn't plan on this either, but I don't want it to end. I know you know what happened, so you know why I had lots of reasons to not want to date. Trust is really hard for me."

Her honesty sliced through me, a sharp blade across the surface of my heart. "I know."

Another wave of relief washed through me. I didn't know what the future held for us, but I knew deep inside that I wanted a chance to give Jade the love she deserved.

"I'm not so great at talking about my feelings," she offered with a sheepish smile.

"No?" I teased. "And here I am, the expert."

After a long moment, she slipped off her stool and stepped between my knees as I turned toward her. "How about we maybe take a break from talking?"

Chapter Twenty-Nine

JADE

I was usually cold at night. Ever since I was a little girl, I'd had a habit of sleeping in my socks because my feet got cold. Lucas used to tease me about it when we were kids.

That's how I knew right off I wasn't alone in my bed when I woke up. I was warm and toasty all over, including my feet, and I didn't even have socks on.

I was plastered against Walker's side with one of my feet tucked between his calves. He had an arm wrapped around my shoulders, holding me firm against him. I didn't mind that one bit. Walker's body was just, well, it was ridiculous. The man was too lucky by half. He was all hard muscle, even when relaxed. Walker was one of those men nature just blessed, perhaps in a moment of boredom, thinking somebody deserved to look like that all over without too much effort.

Opening my eyes, I shifted slightly. I lifted my head and rested my chin on my hand over his chest. I could feel the steady thump of his heart, and his skin was warm under my palm. His dark hair was mussed. I could've presumed it was from sleep, but maybe not. I'd tangled my fingers in his hair when he pushed my knees apart and proceeded to drive me absolutely wild with his mouth hours ago. This man knew how to take care of a woman.

I took a long look at his face in sleep. He had a masculine face with two dark slashes for brows, a bold nose, sculpted cheekbones, and a sexy chin. Dear God, since when did I think a *chin* could be sexy?

Everything about Walker is sexy, my snide voice offered up quickly.

I bit my lip, contemplating his startling announcement last night. Just thinking about it sent my heartbeat off to the races. It unsettled me. I was afraid I felt the same way. My mind kept getting caught on one word—think. *I think I'm falling in love with you.*

Thinking wasn't the same as knowing. While he had said he hadn't expected any of this, it wasn't just that I hadn't expected it. I'd promised myself I would never care so much that it mattered.

As if he somehow sensed my state in his sleep, Walker's legs shifted, and he opened his eyes. When he found me staring at him, his eyes came fully open. "Good morning. I think."

The slow smile that curled his lips sent my heart tripping and stumbling. I swallowed and actually managed a breath, mentally willing myself to stay calm.

"Good morning."

The temptation to kiss him was almost overwhelming. When I felt myself starting to fight it, I consciously decided not to worry so much. I leaned forward and brushed my lips over his, far too gratified when his hand slipped down my spine, and he pulled me closer.

"Mmm. I don't mind waking up, not like this," he murmured when his head fell back.

I straightened, tugging the sheet up with me, only to reveal his obvious arousal. I felt my entire body flush, and I bit my lip as I looked back at him. Unabashed, he shrugged.

"It's nearly a permanent condition around you. Perhaps I should be sorry, but I'm not."

"You don't need to be sorry."

I couldn't say why, but I felt a little embarrassed. My eyes landed on the scar just under his ribs that wrapped around from his back. "What happened here?" I asked, looking for a distraction.

Walker looked down. "Nothing too exciting. I was swinging on a rope into the water one time when I was a kid and it got caught. Gave me a nasty rope burn."

When his eyes met mine again, the moment felt suddenly intimate. Which I suppose it was. Restless, I stood and let the sheet fall away as I strode toward the shower. "I'll make coffee after I shower," I called over my shoulder.

I was just stepping in the shower with steam filling the bathroom when Walker came in. He climbed in right behind me and closed the glass door. "You don't mind company, do you?"

As if I could say no. Not when he was standing in front of me aroused and dipping his head to press a kiss to the side of my neck.

We did manage to shower, but Walker also imprinted himself on me. He pressed me up against the tile when he sank inside of me and brought me to a shattering climax.

We did have coffee after that, and it all felt rather mundane. Meanwhile, I felt like a little fish dropped in a new pool of water. I was swimming around madly trying to make sense of it all. I wasn't unhappy, more like unsettled and uncertain.

After he left to go to work, I was relieved when Dani called asking for some urgent help to cover the bar at the Lodge restaurant after one of their bartenders called out sick. I *seriously* needed the distraction of being busy.

Chapter Thirty

WALKER

I wiped sweat off my brow and turned off the miter saw. Lucas and I had finished the flooring in the other cabin yesterday. I'd left him to put a coat of finish on it and moved onto the next one. As it was, I was alone when my phone blew up with texts and then a phone call.

"It's Walker, what is it?"

"It's Dave. He's going to die."

"What? Who is this?"

"It's Steve, Dave's brother."

My brain felt fuzzy, and I couldn't think. I nonsensically asked, "Are you sure? What happened?"

"He had a stroke and sustained brain damage. He's on life-support, but it's not looking good. If you want to see him, you're gonna want to come now."

I didn't even think. I went through the rote motions of putting away my tools. I walked through the trees to my truck. I wanted to talk to Jade.

I tried calling her, but there was no answer. I couldn't bring myself to leave this kind of message on a voicemail. I texted her instead. *I have to go see Dave. Call me. I'll explain.*

After that, I tried to call Jackson, but got his voicemail and the same for the vet clinic. In a pinch, I left a message with Shay, letting her know I had to leave for a personal emergency and would call with an update as soon as I had one.

I hopped in my truck and hightailed it up to the hospital where Dave was. I suppose I was in shock. Because I had to, I kept my focus with my eyes trained on the road. I was disappointed Jade hadn't called yet when I got there, but I figured she was at work. The moment I walked into the hospital and encountered Dave's mother crying silently in the waiting area outside his room, I forgot everything else.

————

It was dark outside, and Dave's hospital room was cast in shadow. The doctor had told us he was brain dead. I'd demanded they show us the scans. Without the machine breathing for him, he would already be gone from us. Dave's parents had fallen asleep outside in the waiting room and Steve had gone home for the night, reporting he would be back in the morning.

I stared down at Dave, wishing the rhythmic sound of the machine keeping him alive wasn't so loud. It was an ever-present reminder that he was already slipping away. I reached for his hand, curling mine over it. In a way, I was seeking his comfort rather than the other way around.

"What the hell, dude?" I asked. I tried to inject humor in my voice because that was the kind of friendship we had. When things were hard, we gave each other hell.

My chest was tight and sadness rolled through me. I couldn't believe a heart attack had felled this man who'd been strong and healthy, or so it seemed. And now, a stroke came along. Apparently, strokes weren't that uncommon after cardiac surgery.

"I'm gonna fucking miss you."

I released his hand and balled mine in fists. Resting them on the edge of the bed, I bowed my head. Dave and I hadn't seen each other much in the last few years just because of life. Mine took me in one direction, while his took him in another.

Yet, he'd remained one of those friends for me. You know? The ones you can call no matter what. No matter how long it's been since you've talked, it still feels as if you're just picking up from the last conversation. There was never any guilt trip about how come you hadn't called. Our friendship was that solid.

I'd meant to call him anyway to check on how he was doing. I'd also wanted more advice. He and I had spoken regularly since his wedding.

His words from a conversation only days ago echoed through my thoughts. *"It doesn't make sense until it happens. Love, that is. But when it does, you'll know it. Seems to me that might be what's happened with Jade. I bet on it with Jenny."*

He'd offered that last part up with a chuckle.

"How much did you bet?" I'd asked, trying to keep my tone light.

"A hundred bucks and dinner at her favorite restaurant."

"What did Jenny think?"

I could still hear Dave's laugh through the phone line now.

"Well, that was the catch. She agreed with me. She wasn't as convinced as I was that Jade was already falling for you. But she was all on board that you were falling for Jade. In fact, she said, leave it to Walker to fall for a woman who makes him work for it. Don't waste time."

Those were the last three words Dave said to me before he said goodbye.

At the sound of the door to his hospital room opening, I lifted my head to see Jenny. Her eyes were puffy, and her cheeks splotchy.

I stepped away from the bed, turning to face her as she came around the end. "I'd ask how you're doing, but..."

She nodded, sniffling a little and dabbing at her nose with a tissue that had seen better days. "It's okay. Actually, it's not. Not even a little. But, I'll take what little time I've had with him and count it as the blessing it will always be. I know so many people who tell me they never fell in love. I got the real deal. Just not for very long."

She cocked her head to the side, her eyes holding mine, her gaze steady and clear. With every beat of my heart, I ached for her and Dave.

"Dave mentioned you called for some advice about Jade the other day."

I nodded. "Why do you mention that?"

"Because you're a good man, Walker. I hope you follow his advice."

"I will," I replied, my throat tight.

The door opened again, and Dave's parents entered, followed by his brother and the medical team. When I saw the priest filing in behind the others, my heart seized for a minute.

Dave had never been the most devout guy, but he'd been raised Catholic. The hours ticked by, and I could hardly focus on anything except one moment at a time. Dave's mother had second thoughts about taking him off life support, so that was a thing to process.

I was surprised Jenny was so steadfast. However, she was a nurse and told me she knew what those brain scans meant. He was brain dead. Dave had a living will, something he'd set up years back. Although I hated, absolutely *hated*, that he was dying, I knew him. He would not want to live out an indefinite existence hooked up to a machine.

Meanwhile, I didn't even think about anything else, much less where my phone was.

Chapter Thirty-One

JADE

"Oops!"

I looked over to see Rylie had taken about four steps after coming through the front door. She was frozen in place and was presently looking down at the muddy footprints she'd left behind her.

Her wide eyes whipped to mine. "What do I do?"

"Stay right there," I said as I wiped my hands on my apron and hurried from the kitchen into the living room.

I grabbed the rubber shoe tray by the door and set it beside Riley. She put her muddy boots in there and scampered down the hallway to change. I glanced over at the clock above the sink in the kitchen. Lucas and Valentina wouldn't be home from work for several hours.

After returning the shoe tray to its place by the door, I walked back into the kitchen just as Rylie came out from the hallway. "Should we clean it up?" she called as she looked down at her muddy boot prints.

"We'll wait until it dries and then vacuum it up."

"But I want it to be clean before Valentine and Dad get home."

I looked into my niece's earnest face and smiled. "I know. We've got plenty of time."

Rylie gave a last look at the mud and skipped into the kitchen. "What are we making?" she asked when she stepped onto the small stool Lucas had gotten just for her in the kitchen.

She liked to cook with Valentina, and they often did projects together, just like she did with me when I was babysitting.

I pointed to the two eggs on the counter beside a bowl of flour. "You can crack those eggs into the bowl. We're making peanut butter cookies."

I was relieved Valentina had called me in a pinch. She often worked from home, but Shay needed her on short notice for help with an ordering problem. I'd needed something to do. After the other night with Walker and those sleepy sensual moments the following morning, my heart felt full to bursting. Feathering along the edges of my thoughts had been the idea that maybe, just maybe, I could relax and have faith in Walker.

Then, I'd gotten that cryptic text from him. I'd tried calling and texting. And got nothing. We were on day two now, and I still hadn't heard anything from him.

The only conclusion I could come to was Walker must've regretted his insane impulse to tell me he was falling in love with me. Because I was constantly prepared to tolerate the abrupt ripping away of trust, it made perfect sense.

I was a mix of angry, hurt, and painfully disappointed. Because, dammit, I had gone and fallen in love with him like an idiot. Even worse, I'd let myself have faith in him, and in us.

Although it was hard to keep my mind off Walker and just how stupid I'd been, I did my best to throw myself into making cookies with Rylie. If anyone could keep me sort of distracted, she could.

———

I reached for my phone again, spinning it around on the counter and tapping the button to see the screen. Still nothing from Walker. A big, fat nothing.

Apparently, he'd decided he didn't need to explain anything to me after all. "That's just fine," I murmured to myself.

"What's just fine?" Rylie's voice reached me when she appeared from the end of the hallway. She'd been building a fort in her playroom.

"Oh, nothing, sweet pea. Just talking to myself."

Rylie wrinkled her nose as she eyed me. "I know. Are you okay?"

"I'm fine. Just got some things on my mind."

Rylie opened her mouth, and I braced myself for her next question. There was nothing quite like being grilled by a curious seven-year-old.

I was saved by the door opening, and Valentina stepping through. Her arms were laden with grocery bags.

"Let me help you with those." Hallelujah, something else to do. I hurried around the counter.

Rylie trotted over too, and the three of us carried the groceries into the kitchen.

"You're a little early," I commented as we finished putting away the groceries.

Valentina brushed her hair away from her forehead with the back of her wrist and closed the refrigerator. "Oh yeah. It didn't take as long as Shay thought. She's not really a fan of crosschecking things on the spreadsheets. I sent her away and took care of it," Valentina explained with a smile and a shrug. "Lucas is out on a call, so I'm not sure when we can expect him for dinner." She looked down at Rylie. "Now would be about the time JJ asks you to do your homework. Do you want to go to your room and take care of that while we get dinner ready?"

Rylie's braid bounced up and down on her shoulder with her nod. With a little wave, she dashed down the hallway.

Valentina smiled at me. "She loves her new desk. Now she doesn't want to do her homework in the kitchen anymore."

"She's a good kid. Anyway—" I began, just as Valentina spoke at the same time.

"Do you want to stay for some coffee and maybe dinner?" she asked.

I almost hugged her in relief. I was *that* desperate not to have time on my hands. As it was, I wasn't due at the bar for my shift until eight tonight. The hours between now and then yawned before me. That was plenty of time for recrimination and beating myself up over being an idiot about Walker.

"I'd love that!"

My answer must've come across as a bit too enthusiastic because Valentina gave me a quizzical look. I did love hanging out with her and we'd become tight friends, but enthusiasm wasn't really my style.

"I'll make coffee," I volunteered quickly before stepping around her and aiming straight for the coffee maker on the counter. "What are you planning for dinner?"

"I promised Rylie I'd try this new recipe she found. It's basically homemade macaroni and cheese. Lucas will eat anything, and I'm sure it will be good."

She started pulling things out of the refrigerator and cabinets while I started coffee. Once I had the coffee going, I slipped my hips onto a stool across from where Valentina was working on the counter. She shooed me away when I offered to help.

"There's really nothing to this. It's noodles and this melted cheese sauce." After a few quiet moments, Valentina asked, "All right, what's wrong?" She turned on the burner under a pot of water and started shredding cheese.

"What do you mean?" I hedged.

Valentina narrowed her eyes at me and pursed her lips. "I know you well enough to know when you're in a weird mood, and you're definitely in a weird mood. If I had to guess, it's something to do with Walker. Shay mentioned he had some kind of family emergency."

"She did? Does she know what's going on?" My second question practically tripped over the first because it came out so fast.

Valentina arched a brow and cocked her head to the side. "Ah, see, I knew I was right. It's totally something to do with Walker."

I leaned my head down, tunneling my hands through my hair with a sigh before lifting my face to meet her gaze again. "Fine. You're right. He left me this cryptic text saying he had to go see Dave and he'd explain. I don't know what the hell is going on. I haven't heard from him in two days. I feel like an idiot for falling for him, and I don't know what to do. I mean, if it mattered, I think I would've heard from him by now."

Valentina bit her lip as she considered me. "Maybe, maybe not. Since you don't know what's going on, maybe you should try not to assume it's bad."

I let out a heavy sigh just as the coffee maker beeped. Standing, I strode over to fetch two mugs and fill them with coffee. "You know, sometimes you're too optimistic," I commented over my shoulder.

Turning, I set Valentina's mug on the counter beside her before taking a long sip of mine. She glanced sideways as she finished shredding some cheese. "Well, sometimes you're too pessimistic. Especially about men," she said with a pointed look.

———

I considered Valentina's observation as I stared at the drunken guy standing across the bar from me. "No," I said flatly. "You're cut off for the rest of the night. If you keep bugging me about another drink, I'll be kicking you out of the bar."

The guy gave me something between a lopsided smile and a glare. "Geez, you're a bitch for someone so pretty."

And Valentina wondered why I was pessimistic about men. With a disgusted snort, I turned away, immediately taking another drink order from a young woman who was ordering for a table of ten in the corner.

I still hadn't heard a thing from Walker, and it had now been three days since I'd seen him. Much as I wanted to take Valentina's advice to be more optimistic and my oh-so-wishful heart was being needy and noisy, I'd come to the conclusion that his radio silence could only mean one thing. He'd reconsidered his feelings.

I was wondering if I'd seen everything through the wrong lens with him. Maybe he'd been prepping me for the inevitable choice to have one last night and make a clean break of it if I didn't scrounge up the nerve to tell him I loved him. And now, even more obnoxiously, I was probably going to have to come up with some sort of explanation for Lucas, seeing as he'd asked Walker about us. I was surprised he hadn't asked yet, but he'd stayed quiet even though he certainly had a few chances. My best guess about that was Valentina had told him to leave me in peace for the time being.

I tried to ignore the piercing ache in my heart. Fortunately, the bar was busy tonight. The brewery, which was on an adjacent property, was hosting a wedding event this weekend. There was spillover from the guests filling the bar tonight. The downside to this particular crowd was it kept reminding me of the very wedding that had started it all for Walker and me.

I spun through making one drink after another, relieved when Griffin, one of the bartenders at the lodge restaurant who occasionally pitched in here, came in to help out. The pace was relentless.

After the busy night ended, we were cleaning up together and Griffin's voice came over my shoulder when I pulled my phone out of my pocket for probably the thousandth time tonight. "Okay, what gives?"

"Huh?" I asked as I turned and tossed some empty beer bottles into the recycling bin.

"You managed to check your phone in between almost every drink you mixed tonight. I gotta give you credit, though, it didn't slow you down a bit."

I looked over at Griffin. Grabbing one of the clean white towels from a stack behind the bar, I dipped it in a disinfectant mixture and began wiping down the bar. I sure as hell didn't want to admit I kept checking to see if Walker had texted or called.

Griffin chuckled. "I'm guessing it's something to do with your boyfriend."

Pausing, I rested a hand on my hip. "I don't have a boyfriend."

Griffin leveled me with a look. "That's not what I heard."

I groaned. "What did you hear?"

"I heard that fake wedding date turned out to be pretty real."

I practically growled at him before I began vigorously cleaning around the sink behind the bar.

"No need to get so pissed off, Jade," he said. "Speaking of..."

The moment he said that, the hairs on the back of my neck rose and a prickle raced down my spine. I didn't know how I knew, but I knew Walker was here.

I kept my voice low. "Didn't we lock up?"

"In the front. You were supposed to get the back door. How about I finish cleaning up and you, uh, I don't know, go somewhere to talk?" Griffin offered.

I hated that my heart was pounding so hard, each beat

more resounding than the last and coming in rapid succession.

"Hey, Jade."

The sound of Walker's voice struck me right in my solar plexus. Whether I wanted to or not, my head lifted. I found him standing directly across from me on the other side of the bar. He looked tired, his dark hair mussed, and the lines on his face tense.

I finally managed to speak. "Hey."

Before I realized what was happening, Griffin stepped to my side, removing the towel from my hand. "Jade was just finishing up," he said, patting me on the back.

I cast him a glare. He ignored me. "You two want to talk out back? I'll take care of anything left to do and leave out the front."

I didn't know why the hell Griffin was trying to be so freaking helpful when I didn't need any help. Either I made a little scene here in front of him, or I talked to Walker out back. Although Griffin was merely an audience of one, I didn't want to make any kind of scene in front of anyone. I felt too stupid about the whole thing.

I swallowed back a sharp retort. "Sure. Come on back."

I walked out from behind the bar. Walker was standing right there. It felt as if every hair on my body was electrified. I was so attuned to him. Although I was confused and hurt over his complete silence the last few days, I sensed something was very wrong.

Walker didn't say anything and followed me quietly through the door into the back hallway. It swung shut behind us, and I walked halfway down, my anxiety driving me forward more than anything. Uncertain where to go, I went into a storage room, which held shelves of beer and liquor.

When I turned to face Walker, he stopped about a foot away from me and stuffed his hands in his pockets. "Dave died."

Shock hit me. "Oh my God! What happened? Why didn't you tell me?"

"He had a stroke. It affected the part of his brain that controls breathing. He lost air long enough he was brain dead. Apparently, having a stroke is a common complication from cardiac surgery."

"Oh, Walker, I'm so sorry."

Those last three words felt so incredibly inadequate. Yet, there were no words adequate enough to capture that loss. I didn't realize I'd stepped closer to him until I felt my hand sliding down his forearm in a caress. His eyes searched my face before he cleared his throat and took a ragged breath.

"I lost my phone," he added. My anger and swirling confusion dissipated instantly. "I tried to call before I left, but it didn't feel right to say that on a message. When I couldn't get a hold of you, I just had to go." He paused, and the sound of his swallow was audible in the quiet room. "They took him off life support this morning after another long night. His mother kind of flipped out, so it delayed the decision."

I suddenly felt terrible about my anger and doubt. Dave was Walker's closest friend. I couldn't imagine the sense of loss he was feeling and wished I'd been able to be there with him.

"I'm really, really sorry, Walker." I placed my hand over his heart, feeling the steady beat of it underneath my touch.

He nodded slowly before lifting a hand and brushing a wayward lock of hair behind my ear. "I understand if you'd rather not, but I was wondering if you'd go to the funeral with me."

"Of course I will."

I felt his heartbeat kick up as he regarded me. After a moment, his eyes fell closed, and he bowed his head slightly. I waited, because it was the only thing to do.

When he lifted his head, his eyes immediately locked

with mine—the look there was intense and piercing. My own heartbeat started to drum wildly.

"The other night, I meant to say something, and I chickened out," he said. His mouth curled at one corner with a sheepish smile.

"You? I find that hard to believe."

I meant that, I truly did. Because Walker was many things, but a coward wasn't one of them.

His heartbeat drummed under my palm, and I sensed he was nervous. My heart responded in kind, picking up its pace until I felt a little breathless.

He nodded slowly. "I talked to Dave that day, and he told me not to be an idiot."

"About what?"

"I only said I *thought* I was falling for you. That wasn't the whole truth. There's no more falling. Hell, I've already crash-landed. I *know* I'm in love with you."

His words shocked me. My heart stopped beating, and my breath seized as I stared at him. Then, my heart lunged, like a celebratory song of joy burst through me.

My mouth must've fallen open because Walker stepped closer, pressing two fingers under my chin. "You seem surprised. Let me make it completely clear. I never expected to fall in love with anyone. I know maybe you don't return the feeling. You did, after all, tell me you didn't even date. If I had more sense, I would've realized it that very first weekend on our fake date. I. Love. You. Everything about you. Including your attitude and the way you challenge me. I can't imagine life without you, and when I realized that, I called Dave for some advice." Sadness flickered in Walker's eyes, but he forged ahead.

All the while, every word tattooed itself across my heart, stripping away my defenses, the joy so intense it hurt a little. Because, in all honesty, not only was I afraid to trust, but I was afraid to love. These last few days terrified me because

I'd gone and fallen so hard for Walker that I didn't know how to ever make it back.

"So, I chickened out what I meant to tell you and only half-said it. The last few days have been shit, and I still can't quite believe it. But, I'm not gonna wait to honor the last advice Dave gave me. I know maybe you're not ready, but—"

My words burst forth, interrupting him swiftly. "I am ready. I guess I'm a chicken too." I hadn't even scrambled up the nerve. Everything felt as if it were spinning inside of me, a swirl of emotion with all of my old fears tangling into it. On the heels of a deep breath, I finally let my heart speak. "I love you. Maybe I don't date, but I'll date you."

I didn't realize I'd started crying until I felt Walker's thumb under one of my eyes and felt the cool path of the teardrop smear over my cheek as he brushed it away. "Hey, don't cry," he murmured.

I smiled and felt like an idiot. "They're not sad tears. I promise I'm just—" I circled my hand in the air. "Overwhelmed, I guess."

His eyes held mine for a blurry moment before he dipped his head and brought his lips to mine. Our kiss started out gentle, almost careful. The moment I sighed and his tongue tangled sensually with mine, it went from gentle to deep and searching. Suddenly, we were frantic.

For me, it was a combination of the piercing emotional ache of the last few days—no matter how misplaced—and the reckoning with my own feelings. My fierce need and emotion intensified with learning his best friend, who'd only married weeks prior, had died. I needed to lose myself in Walker, to dive into the flames and know I would come out on the other side with him.

I didn't remember much, other than piercing sensations burning through me. Somehow, we were only half-dressed. Walker spun with me in his arms and pressed my back against the wall. With enough force, the shelf beside us shook. The clinking of boxes of wine, beer, and liquor punctured my awareness.

My jeans were hanging off one leg, and Walker had shoved my panties to the side. The rough denim of his jeans abraded the insides of my thighs. The underside of his velvety, hot shaft slid through the slick juices of my arousal.

I stared into his eyes, and my heart gave a sure, steady thump—as if in recognition of this moment, *this* man, and how he'd become so much of everything to me.

"I love you," he whispered, just before adjusting the angle of his hips and surging into me in one stroke.

I cried out at the sense of fullness, and the fusion of our bodies together. Forcing my eyes open again, I pressed a kiss to his lips. "I love you too. I didn't mean to, but there's no going back now."

Walker's lips curled in a slow grin. The look in his eyes was intimate and a little dirty, sending my belly spinning in flips. "There's definitely no going back."

Our coupling was rushed and messy. My climax burst through me, shattering me inside and out as I felt the heat of his release filling me.

Chapter Thirty-Two

WALKER

I pulled myself together quickly after we heard the door to the hallway opening. Jade had been as frantic as me, but she now stood before me fully dressed. Her cheeks were flushed, her hair was a tousled mess, and her lips were puffy from our kisses. She stared at me, her stunning green eyes wide and vulnerable.

"Who the hell is that?" I whispered. I'd slammed the door to this room shut in a hot second once we heard footsteps coming our way.

"Griffin must've forgotten something. If it was anybody else, they would've wondered why you slammed the door." She sagged against the wall when we heard the door close again. "Can we go home now?"

"Of course. Is home your place or mine?" I reached for her hand, reeling her to me.

She relaxed into my embrace easily. She tucked her head against my shoulder and took a deep breath. "It doesn't matter. I just want to be where you are."

My heart felt cracked wide-open. Jade's presence filled all the cracked spaces, and I would never be the same.

"In that case, let's go to your place. I left in a rush, so I'm not sure if my bed is made, or if I have anything decent for food."

Jade lifted her head, peering up at me. She placed her hand over my heart again, her gaze sobering. "I'm so very sorry about Dave."

"So am I." I curled my hand over hers. Although the loss of Dave would be with me always, Jade would help ease the ache of it.

———

I leaned against the reception desk in the vet clinic, watching as Everett walked with his crooked gait across the floor. When he reached us, he sniffed my feet, looking up expectantly.

Glancing at Shay, I commented, "He seems to want something."

Shay cast a sheepish smile over her shoulder. "I may have been a bit too generous with the treats." She handed me a treat that looked to be compressed fruits and nuts over the counter.

Leaning down, I held it out on my palm and Everett grabbed it with both paws. After he ate it, he wandered off to investigate the magazine basket in the corner.

The main door opened, and Jade came walking through. Her cheeks were flushed, and her hair was pulled into a ponytail with loose strands falling around her face.

"Oh my God," she said with a sigh as she reached my side. "It's soooo hot out."

"According to my weather app, the heat index is 105," Shay called over her shoulder.

Jade rested her hips against the counter. We were still adjusting to the state of our relationship. Or rather, I should say, the reality that we loved each other and even had a relationship.

My prickly, guarded, and feisty Jade had a smile teasing in the corners of her mouth and a glint in her eyes. I leaned over. "Hey," I whispered right before I brushed my lips over hers.

Just that subtle touch sent electricity zinging through my body. I was becoming accustomed to a state of almost constant anticipation when I was around her.

While I was orienting to my feelings for Jade and her presence in my life, I was still adjusting to Dave's passing. It had been almost a month since he died. I missed him so much, and a part of me almost kept forgetting he was gone. Since we hadn't seen each other daily for years, I was accustomed to not seeing him on a regular basis. I'd think of something I wanted to mention to him, and then I'd have to remind myself he was gone. Although Dave's death was a huge blow, Jade was a quiet, steady light in my life.

When I lifted my head, I saw Shay smiling at us. "Hey, Jade," she said cheerily.

Jade's cheeks flushed slightly, and she sighed. "Hey." When Shay kept on grinning, she added, "It was just a kiss. You don't have to look so excited."

Shay shrugged. "I know, but I love it. You swore off men, and now you're totally into Walker."

Jade glanced over at Everett, who had climbed on one of the waiting room chairs and was looking out the window toward the parking lot. "So what's the plan for him?"

Nimble though he was, he had a distinct limp and didn't move very quickly. If he were left out in the wild, he wouldn't fare too well. Shay leaned against the counter opposite us. "For now, he'll stay here. There aren't too many rescue programs that will take opossums."

Jade knelt down and tapped her fingers on the floor. He came walking over, and she scratched between his ears before he meandered to investigate yet another corner of the waiting room.

Lucas came through the front entrance. Lucas and I had

eventually had that conversation about Jade, which ended with a stern warning from him. In essence, he said he'd hurt me if I hurt Jade. Those weren't his exact words, but I got the point.

He had nothing to worry about. As it was, Dave's final words to me and my eventual facing up to just what Jade meant to me had opened a dam. My entire world revolved around her now. That was perfectly all right with me.

Lucas stopped beside us, glancing down with a bemused smile when Everett came over to sniff his boots. He glanced from me to Jade. "Are you here to check on this guy?"

Jade gave him a pointed look. "Yes. Isn't that why you're here?"

Lucas chuckled. "No. I'm just here to pick up Valentina."

"Of course. You need me to babysit tomorrow, right?"

"That'd be great. We need to push through on a few of those cabins because Jackson would like to have them ready for booking, so I plan to work late." Lucas caught my eyes and rolled his slightly. "And, Valentina wants to run to Asheville to do some shopping."

"We'll finish up this weekend," I said. "We'll have to wrangle a few of the other guys to help, but we can make it happen."

"Please do," Shay chimed in. "We've got a waitlist for reservations right now."

"I'll be there by eight tomorrow morning," Jade said.

Lucas nodded and turned to walk down the hallway. "Catch y'all later."

"You ready to go?" I asked.

"Where are y'all going?" Shay interjected.

"Home," Jade and I said simultaneously.

"That's when I know you're in love. When you both say home, and it doesn't matter where it is," Shay said with a slow smile.

EPILOGUE

Jade

Approximately two years later

"Come on," Valentina urged as she slid her hand through my elbow and tugged me forward.

"I don't like surprises," I muttered.

"Really? I never would've noticed." Valentina rolled her eyes, her tone dry as she persisted in pulling me along with her.

"It would help if you told me where we were going." I planted my feet firmly until she stopped.

Her brows knitted, and she rested a hand on her hip. "You're more stubborn than Lucas."

"You called?" Lucas's voice came from behind us.

Turning, I watched my brother approach us. "What the hell? Why in the world are you also going for some random hike?"

Valentina had showed up at the house I shared with Walker this morning and insisted she needed me to come somewhere with her. Then, she drove us to Stolen Hearts

Lodge and had me tromping through the woods and fields on a hike. We were well beyond the area where the resort and rescue program were located.

Lucas stopped beside us, the hint of understanding and amusement held in his eyes making me a little restless and anxious. "What's going on?" I pressed.

"Come on. It's a party," Lucas replied.

Before I could reply, he had me by the other elbow. Between the two of them, they were moving me ahead and not giving me much choice in the matter.

"Do I need to call Walker for a rescue?"

"I doubt it," was all I got from Lucas.

Valentina was looking steadfastly forward. My guess was if I asked her enough questions, she would break. Valentina was the absolute worst liar I'd ever met in my life. It was nearly impossible for her to lie, even when it was for a good cause.

"Come on, Valentina," I cajoled, giving her a little nudge with my elbow. "Tell me what's going on. I don't think the surprise has something to do with Shay, or you'd tell me about it."

Valentina closed her lips in a tight line, but she still refused to look at me. My brother simply shrugged. "You're not gonna get a thing out of me."

We passed through another copse of trees and came into a clearing where a picturesque chapel sat on a hillside. My feet stopped moving, and my heartbeat echoed throughout my entire body as butterflies spun wildly in my belly. "What's going on?" I asked, my voice sounding a little shaky.

Valentina finally looked at me. "Walker has a surprise for you."

"Here?" That single word came out in a squeak. "What is this place? I've never been here."

Lucas began moving again, and I was too stunned to stop him from pulling me forward. In another moment, we'd reached a tiny chapel. Walking up the stone steps, Lucas opened the heavy wooden double doors, which led directly into the space. There were rows of seating on either side. I peered between Lucas and Valentina. "How come I've never seen this place before?"

Valentina answered, "Jackson's great-grandparents built this chapel over a hundred years ago. It's lovely, isn't it? Over here." She tugged me to the side where there was a doorway. She practically shoved me through the door and shut it behind me.

Walker was standing by a window in the small square room. It had white walls and glossy wide plank flooring. He turned to look at me. The sunlight splashing through the window glinted on his dark locks as his gaze snagged mine from across the room.

My heart was pounding so hard, it felt as if my entire being was nothing more than a heartbeat. When he caught my eyes, I felt myself smiling. If only because Walker had that effect on me. His lips quirked at the corners as he took several steps to close the distance between us.

"Um, what's going on, Walker?"

I didn't realize my hands were cold until the warmth of his grip enveloped mine. I was nervous, unaccountably so.

"You said you'd marry me," he began in that slow, gravelly drawl that never failed to send heat spinning like fire through my veins. It didn't matter that it had been two years since I finally fessed up to my feelings for Walker. It didn't matter that he asked me to marry him almost a year ago now. It didn't matter that I saw him every day. His effect on me remained potent. Nothing faded. Instead of time dulling the force of my reaction to him, it seemed to sharpen it.

"I did. See?" Freeing my left hand, I held it up and wiggled my fingers.

Walker had gotten me a gorgeous engagement ring set with an opal, which happened to be my favorite stone.

He dipped his head, leaning his forehead against mine. "I

do see. But you keep putting off the actual wedding. So, I decided to make it happen. You can call it off, though."

He lifted his head and watched me quietly. I bit my lip, staring at him and feeling my cheeks get hot. "I don't want to call it off. I just hate"—I paused, waving in the air randomly—"things where lots of people are paying attention to me," I explained.

"I know. That's exactly why we're having it here where it's just the people that matter. Everyone will be here in fifteen minutes. Your parents and your brother, Rylie, my mom, and our friends here. If you want to run away, go ahead. No one is allowed to give you any hell about it."

I stared into his smoky eyes and my heart went thump, thump, thump, thump. I couldn't believe he'd planned this. Trust was something that was still hard for me. Oh, I trusted Walker. Completely. But I didn't quite trust that I deserved him.

I looked down at my jeans and white blouse before bringing my eyes back to his. "I don't have a wedding dress."

"I don't care. I just love you, and I want to make it official."

So it was that Walker and I got married in a tiny chapel looking out over Stolen Hearts Valley. It was the kind of weather someone who put a lot of work into planning a wedding would've paid money for—clear skies with puffy clouds, and a soft breeze on a warm spring day.

I'd been spared all the planning. With Walker orchestrating it, our friends showed up to celebrate with us. Hours later, I held a glass of champagne up and tapped it against Walker's. "To us," he said.

Then, he swept me into a kiss that shouldn't have been public.

WALKER

Another two years later, or thereabouts

Leaning down, I grazed my teeth lightly over one of Jade's nipples. It puckered tightly under my mouth, and she let out a sharp cry.

"Please, Walker." She gasped as she bucked her hips against me. "Hurry," she urged, curling her legs around my hips.

The slick tease of her core against the underside of my cock proved to be too much for my control. On the heels of another breath, I drew back and sheathed myself in her channel, savoring her silky, slick, and clenching fit.

"I don't wanna rush," I murmured as I lifted my head and opened my eyes.

Jade's dark hair was spread out across the pillows, and her eyes flashed with desire. "We have twins. All we get are quickies," she said with a sly grin as she arched into me.

Within minutes, my release was building, and I watched through heavy eyes as she flew apart.

Jade was the touchstone in my world. She was still feisty, she still swore too much, and it would always take a bit for her to let go. As she shattered, my own release followed swiftly before I collapsed against her and rolled us over so my weight didn't crush her.

I thought—silly me—that we might have a few stolen moments. We got maybe two. But they were the best moments. With Jade warm and soft as she rested against me, her skin dewy from our rushed coupling, all felt perfectly right with the world.

But then, it always did when I was with Jade like this— our defenses gone, and nothing but the deep intimacy that bound us tighter and tighter together over time. For a man who once wasn't so sure that I'd ever fall in love, Jade had turned me into the worst sap of all.

My breath was just returning to normal when a thin cry came through the baby monitor on the nightstand beside our bed. Jade laughed softly against my shoulder, the feel of her breath tickling my skin slightly.

"Well, that took longer than I thought," she said when she lifted her head, resting her chin on her hand directly above my heart.

I felt my lips kick into a smile. I lifted my hand to smooth it over her hair. "That might've been almost two whole minutes."

There was another cry. "There goes Dave" she commented.

Our twins were a handful. When Jade first got pregnant three months after we got married, I'd been a bundle of anxiety. Then, we found out we were having twins. Everything felt heightened when there were two. While twins *were* more work, logistically speaking, we'd learned they often comforted each other. That was a secret parents of twins often didn't share. We waited, both of us turning to look at the monitor. Another cry from Dave came before Rachel made a cooing sound, and then they were giggling. At nine months old, they were a handful, but I wouldn't change anything for a second. We'd named our boy after my friend Dave. I had faith our Dave would live up to Dave's memory.

Jade smiled. I squeezed her bottom. At that moment, my stomach let out a growl. Jade eyed me. "We forgot to have dinner first."

I shrugged. "The twins were asleep." That explained everything.

Sleep became more valuable than platinum when you had two babies under the age of one. I'd been warned by my friends who had kids that I should be prepared to live on only a few hours of sleep until at least the age of three and potentially later.

Shifting upward, I propped myself against the head-board, not quite ready to give up this moment with Jade. "How was your day?"

With the sounds of our twins mumbling to each other in garbled speech as background noise through the baby monitor, Jade told me just how her day went.

After feeling like she was floundering with what to do, she'd finally started her own landscaping business as she'd originally wanted years before. She loved working outside and loved flowers. With Valentina's help, she got all the business and accounting details lined out.

Meanwhile, I was still on the first responder crew and still working at the lodge, and it suited me. When I had free time, I was working on building our new house. We still lived in the house I'd inherited from my grandmother, but we needed more space.

My stomach growled again, and Jade rose up. "You're starving. Now that the twins are awake, let's go eat."

An hour or so later, Jade was leaning down to pick up the bits of granola that had fallen on the floor, thrown off by Rachel from her high chair tray. I'd just made a pot of coffee and took a sip and watched her.

My heart clenched. Each beat felt like a burst of joy. Jade stood and tossed the granola in the compost bin under the sink before resting her hips against the counter beside me. I looked down at her messy hair and simply smiled.

"What?" she asked.

"You're beautiful."

"With applesauce on my face," she said, gesturing to the streak on her cheek and then pointing to more on her collarbone, both spread there by Rachel, who was a messy eater.

Dave squealed in the background, his feet thumping against the high chair legs. The cacophony of twins was the backdrop of our life, and I loved every minute of it with Jade.

"Yes, applesauce and all."

Her eyes widened slightly, a slow smile unfurling. "Well, you look amazing with this." She lifted a hand to trail it over my chin. I reached up to feel a dried smear there. "Should we have a moratorium on applesauce?" she teased.

"I don't care about messes with you," I murmured right before dipping my head and bringing my lips to hers.

———

Thank you for reading If We Dare - I hope you loved Jade & Walker's story!

Up next in the Swoon Series is Steal My Heart. All bets are off when Mack unexpectedly crosses paths with his best friend's little sister.

Ash is off limits. Totally. They're just friends, so no problem, right? *Soooo* wrong.

Mack can't stop thinking about her, and he definitely can't stop wanting her.

Ash wants nothing to do with men, most certainly not all-alpha Mack. Except there's one problem. He has a new ability to set her on fire with nothing more than a look.

This friends to lovers, forbidden romance is panty-melting hot, intense & swoon-worthy!

Keep reading for a sneak peek!

Be sure to sign up for my newsletter for the latest news, teasers & more! Click here to sign up: http://jhcroixauthor.com/subscribe/

EXCERPT: STEAL MY HEART

Ash

I swung my guitar over my shoulder and stepped onto the wooden stage, casting a quick smile at the smattering of applause and whistles. "Hey y'all, I'm only here for an hour, so let's not wait."

I never waited. I launched into my first song and got lost in the music. An hour later, I walked off the stage with the cheers from the audience reverberating through me. For that hour, I'd dropped into the one place where I could forget the mess of my life.

"Great set," a voice called, just as someone else's hand slapped my ass, much harder than I preferred from anyone, much less a stranger. I cast a sharp glare over my shoulder and kept on walking. I hoped I had enough tips from filling in at the bar earlier to pad the measly paycheck I would get for playing that set.

"Ash," a voice said, slicing through the din of noise and bodies crowding around me as I tried to get to the back of the bar.

I knew that voice, but for the life of me, I couldn't place

it. I did a quick scan around me. The crowd parted as a tall form became visible. The man practically swatted people out of his way as if they were nothing more than flies.

Mack Blair, all six feet and five inches of him, came into my line of sight. My body did a startling thing with my belly flipping quickly and my pulse doing a little hop, skip, and jump.

Okay, that was weird. Giving myself a mental shake, I smiled up at Mack when he stopped in front of me. "Well, hey there, Mack. What are you doing here?"

Mack's dark blue eyes swept up and down my body before searching my face. "I could ask you the same. Let's—"

I was cut off when someone bumped into me from behind, sending me colliding against Mack. Mack, with his bear-like presence, swiftly slid his arm around my back, shielding me from everyone jostling around us. "Fuck, this place is busy," he muttered.

I'd known Mack for pretty much forever. Since elementary school, at least. I was startled at the little shiver that chased over my skin at the sound of his gruff words in my ear.

"It is," I murmured in reply. "Come on, my stuff is in the back."

Mack kept his arm around my waist, basically clearing a path for us until we reached the door where I pointed. Once we pushed through the door and it swung shut behind us, his arm fell away, and I sagged against the wall.

"Wow, it went from kind of busy to a little nuts while I was playing."

I'd hugged my guitar to my chest while we walked through the crowd, so I lowered it now, holding it loosely in one hand.

Mack gave me a long look. "Good to see you, Ash."

One side of his mouth kicked up into a familiar grin, and my belly did another flip. I wondered just what in the world was going on with this reaction to Mack. I'd never responded to him like this.

"You too. I'd say let's grab a drink here, but it's pretty crowded."

"I drove past a diner down the road. Grab your stuff, and let's go get coffee or food or whatever," Mack commented.

"Sounds good. I'm actually starving," I replied as I pushed off the wall. "Follow me."

Mack and I had grown up in Stolen Hearts Valley, North Carolina, and he was one of my brother's best friends. Awareness prickled down my spine as he followed me down the hallway. I chose to ignore it, convinced my body's weird reaction to him was probably just because I was so startled to see him.

Stepping into the room where the bar owner had told me I could leave my stuff, I grabbed my purse and my bag before I looked up at him. "Jesus. I forgot how tall you were."

Mack arched a brow. "I've been this tall since my senior year in high school. Speaking of forgetting, I forgot how good you were."

"At what?" I countered as I looked at the envelope sitting on top of my purse. I ripped it open to see the check for tonight, a whopping one hundred and fifty bucks, and the cash from my tips.

"Singing and playing," Mack replied.

I held his eyes for a few beats, feeling heat on my cheeks. "Thanks," I finally managed.

I quickly counted out the tips, relieved to discover an additional one hundred bucks.

"You ready?" he asked as I stuffed the envelope in my purse.

"Yup. Let's roll."

Moments later when we stepped out into the parking lot, his gaze slid to mine as he stopped outside the door. "Do you want to follow me to the diner?"

Aaannnnd, here came the first awkward moment. "If you don't mind, I'll hitch a ride with you."

I saw the questions swirling in his eyes and held my breath. "Of course. Come on." Mack gestured with his chin in a general direction.

Relieved he didn't ask anything else yet, I walked beside him as we crossed the parking lot to where he'd parked an all-black SUV in the far corner.

Because he was Mack and a gentleman, even if a bit rough around the edges, he insisted on taking my guitar and bag from me and setting it carefully in the back. He even made sure my guitar case was properly situated so it wouldn't bounce around too much. He also insisted on getting the door for me and wouldn't even close it until I buckled my seat belt.

"I forgot how stubborn you were," I said when he climbed into the driver's seat beside me.

"Ditto. Why the hell don't you have a car, Ash?"

Oh, fuck.

I silently groaned. So much for no questions.

"Can we go to the diner first? I'd like to some food in me before we get into all that."

"Absolutely."

It might've been a few years since I'd actually seen Mack, but I was relieved he had the same steady, easygoing manner. Not much got to Mack, and he wasn't particularly nosy either. That said, I knew I couldn't keep the truth from him.

———

"No. You're coming with me, Ash," Mack said firmly as if he expected me to simply do what he said.

Actually, there was no *as if* here. He fully expected me to do what he said. God, I just freaking *loved* getting bossed around by a man. Not.

I felt myself beginning to clench my teeth and

consciously relaxed them as I glared right back at him. "You don't get to tell me what to do."

Mack took a sip of his coffee, never once breaking his gaze from mine. He was used to people doing what he said. For one, he was usually bigger than anyone else, including most men. The other was he carried himself with this authoritative manner, and people generally did his bidding. He also had this whole rescue complex vibe and never did have enough sense to leave well enough alone.

"Mack, I'm not somebody you need to rescue. I'm fine, and I'll figure it out."

"You're not fine. You're broke, and you have a no car. Apparently, you're planning to try to get back to Stolen Hearts Valley by hitchhiking with your freaking beloved guitar. Have you lost your goddamn mind?"

A flush raced up my neck and into my cheeks. I tried to beat back the defensiveness choking me. "I made it all the way from Colorado to Wyoming with no trouble."

"In case you haven't looked at a map lately, sugar, Wyoming is north of Colorado, so now you're farther away. Stolen Hearts is east of Colorado, not north. Does Jackson know about this grand plan?"

The moment he said my older brother's name out loud, I thought the top of my head might fly off.

MACK

Ash Stone stared at me from across the table. She was pissed. Her cheeks were pink, and her blue eyes were flashing. Damn, she was gorgeous when she was mad.

"Ash, I'm not joking. It's not safe for you."

"And why's that? Because I'm a woman?" she retorted, lifting a napkin from the table and spinning it between her fingers until she twisted it into a knot. "I can take care of myself."

"Ash, please be sensible. Ride with me. Consider that your adventure if that's what you're after."

Ash's eyes looked like the sky on a stormy day just before thunder rumbled and lightning split the sky wide open. After a moment, her gaze fell from mine, and I didn't miss the way her shoulders curled inward. I'd known Ash for as long as I could remember. I knew she was tired, and worry was emanating from her in waves. I didn't know exactly what the hell happened for her to be without a car and hitch-hiking home on her own, but I wasn't leaving her here.

When her gorgeous eyes lifted again and her gaze met mine, a prickle of awareness sizzled down my spine. Okay, that was strange. If you'd asked me before how I felt about Ash, I'd have said she was like a sister. Except nothing about the way my body was reacting to her felt sisterly now. Not even a little. Her brother was one of my closest friends. Growing up, my younger sisters hung out with Ash all the time. On any given week, we were bouncing between houses, close enough that she felt like family.

When I'd looked up and seen her on that stage earlier, she'd taken my breath away as she belted out song after country song. Once the initial shock of seeing her passed, I expected my body's hyper-awareness to fade, but it wasn't fading. Not at all.

"Do you want to tell me what the hell happened, Ash?" I pressed.

———

Coming August 2020!
Steal My Heart

. . .

If you love hot, small town romance, take a visit to Willow Brook, Alaska in my Into The Fire Series. Check out Burn For Me - a second chance romance for the ages. It's FREE on all retailers! Don't miss Cade & Amelia's story!

Go here to sign up for information on new releases: http:// jhcroixauthor.com/subscribe/

FIND MY BOOKS

Thank you for reading If We Dare! I hope you enjoyed the story. If so, you can help other readers find my books in a variety of ways.

1) Write a review!

2) Sign up for my newsletter, so you can receive information about upcoming new releases & receive a FREE copy of one of my books: http://jhcroixauthor.com/subscribe/

3) Like and follow my Amazon Author page at https://amazon.com/author/jhcroix

4) Follow me on Bookbub at https://www.bookbub.com/authors/j-h-croix

5) Follow me on Instagram at https://www.instagram.com/jhcroix/

6) Like my Facebook page at https://www.facebook.com/jhcroix

———

Swoon Series

This Crazy Love

Wait For Me

Break My Fall

Truly Madly Mine

Still Go Crazy

If We Dare

Steal My Heart - coming August 2020!

Into The Fire Series

Burn For Me

Slow Burn

Burn So Bad

Hot Mess

Burn So Good

Sweet Fire

Play With Fire

Melt With You

Burn For You

Crash & Burn

Brit Boys Sports Romance

The Play

Big Win

Out Of Bounds

Play Me

Naughty Wish

Diamond Creek Alaska Novels

When Love Comes

Follow Love

Love Unbroken

Love Untamed

Tumble Into Love

Christmas Nights

Last Frontier Lodge Novels

Take Me Home

Love at Last

Just This Once

Falling Fast
Stay With Me
When We Fall
Hold Me Close
Crazy For You
Just Us
Catamount Lion Shifters
Protected Mate
Chosen Mate
Fated Mate
Destined Mate
A Catamount Christmas
The Lion Within
Lion Lost & Found

ACKNOWLEDGMENTS

Hugs & kisses to my readers. Thank you for still taking a chance on my stories, for your kind notes, for cheering on my books, and for being generally awesome. I couldn't do this without you.

Najla Qamber has made magic with the covers for this series, and I'm so grateful. Much gratitude to my editor for pushing me with every story. Terri D. takes a microscope to my stories and is gracious and kind every step of the way.

To my last line of defense - Janine, Beth P., Terri E., Heather H., Carolyne B., Andrea R. & Lynne E.

To my family for supporting me in everything I do. To my dogs for unconditional love and reminding me what really matters every single day.

The world has faced more than one crisis lately, and it's a strange, sad and anxious time. In the midst of feeling worried, I try to remember we are all in this together. We may be riding out the storm in different places and in different ways, but we can be there for each other by cultivating hope and being kind. I hope my stories give readers a way to escape for a little while. I feel beyond blessed for my readers, for the opportunity to write, and for the kindness that makes the world a better place.

Let's keep taking care of each other.

xoxo

J.H. Croix

ABOUT THE AUTHOR

USA Today Bestselling Author J. H. Croix lives in a small town in the historical farmlands of Maine with her husband and two spoiled dogs. Croix writes contemporary romance with sassy women and alpha men who aren't afraid to show some emotion. Her love for quirky small-towns and the characters that inhabit them shines through in her writing. Take a walk on the wild side of romance with her bestselling novels!

Places you can find me:
jhcroixauthor.com
jhcroix@jhcroix.com

f facebook.com/jhcroix
🐦 twitter.com/jhcroix
📷 instagram.com/jhcroix
BB bookbub.com/authors/j-h-croix

Made in the USA
Monee, IL
14 November 2020

47557491R00141